'Louisa—' His voice was rough. 'Stop looking at me like that. You did it the other day in Resus.'

She swallowed hard. 'Sorry.'

His eyes drifted to her mouth. 'I'm not your type, remember?'

Her heart was pounding against her chest. 'What would you say if I told you I might have been wrong about that?'

There was a long, aching silence, and then finally his eyes lifted to hers. 'I'd say that we'd both be in trouble.'

'Why?'

He gave a crooked smile and brushed her cheek with his fingers. 'Because you want happy ever after and that's one thing I don't do. Go to bed, Louisa. And lock your door.'

Dear Reader

To have loyal and loving family and friends around you is perhaps the greatest gift of all—and who makes a better friend than a brother?

Men don't always talk about problems in the way that women do, but that doesn't make the bond any less powerful, and that's certainly the case with Mac and Josh Sullivan. They work side by side as consultants in a busy A and E department in a rugged part of Cornwall. Their story starts at Christmas.

Mac is the older and the more serious of the two brothers, and Christmas is always a difficult time for him. His life is a mess and Josh decides it's time to do something about that. So he arranges a present with a difference. Louisa. For one month she'll sort out Mac's life. But when Christmas is over, is he really going to let this amazing girl walk out of his life?

For **Josh's** story the weather warms up and we move into summer. A fun-loving playboy, Josh is very different from his brother. He loves his fast car, his boats and his surfboard and, of course, his women! Why would he want to settle down, have children and risk losing all that? But then his new neighbour arrives, along with her six-year-old boy, and Josh is forced to rethink his whole life.

The great thing about being a writer is that you get to interfere with people's lives, and I had a lot of fun seeing Mac finally happy and Josh well and truly tamed by a woman and her child. I hope you enjoy their stories.

Love
Sarah
xxxxx

Look out next month for the second story in
The Cornish Consultants duo
GIFT OF A FAMILY from Mills & Boon®
Medical Romance™

THE NURSE'S CHRISTMAS WISH

BY
SARAH MORGAN

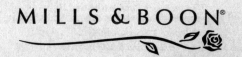

MILLS & BOON®

All the characters in this book have no existence outside the imagination of the author, and have no relation whatsoever to anyone bearing the same name or names. They are not even distantly inspired by any individual known or unknown to the author, and all the incidents are pure invention.

First published in Great Britain 2005
Harlequin Mills & Boon Limited,
Eton House, 18-24 Paradise Road, Richmond, Surrey TW9 1SR

© Sarah Morgan 2005

ISBN 0 263 84339 4

Set in Times Roman 10½ on 12¼ pt.
03-1105-43529

Printed and bound in Spain
by Litografia Rosés, S.A., Barcelona

PROLOGUE

'YOU'RE going to love me. I've solved all your problems.'

'I don't have any problems.' *He had hundreds of problems.* Mac Sullivan tucked the phone under his ear and carried on sifting through the pile of post he'd scooped from the mat just before the phone had rung. He'd only been at the hospital for two days and yet the door would barely open. Where the hell had it all come from? He turned his attention to the phone call. 'And if this is the point where you tell me you've fixed me up with another blind date then I ought to warn you that I'm leaving the country. If you weren't my brother I'd have knocked your teeth down your throat before now.'

'Wouldn't be the first time,' Josh said easily, 'but in this case it would be the wrong move. It's not a blind date. But I have chosen you a *great* Christmas present.'

Mac binned the post without opening it and strolled through to the kitchen, the phone still tucked under his ear. He winced at the mess. The remains of a take-away lay dried up and congealing in foil containers and unwashed dishes were stacked on every available surface.

'I don't need a Christmas present, I need a house-keeper,' he muttered, glancing towards the overflowing bin with something close to desperation. 'Or a

5

brother who clears up after himself. Why doesn't someone invent a bin that empties itself?'

'Last time I looked, ours *was* emptying itself,' Josh said mildly, 'mostly over the kitchen floor. And housekeepers always leave because they fall in love with you. Personally I find you a moody, sarcastic bastard but for some inexplicable reason women seem to find that irresistible. You need to smile more and cut out the brooding, Heathcliffe look and maybe they could concentrate on looking after the house.'

Choosing to ignore his brother's remarks, Mac flicked on the kettle and hunted in vain for a clean mug. 'I'm putting in another advert.'

'It's Christmas in less than two weeks,' Josh reminded him. 'Everyone is shopping and cooking and decorating the house with lights. They don't want to come and clear up our mess. No, in the short term we're in trouble. But in the long term, you need to get married again. That would solve everything.'

Married?

Mac closed his eyes and the breath hissed through his teeth. 'I don't think so.

He was better off alone.

There was a brief silence on the other end of the phone. 'You can't lock yourself away for ever,' Josh said softly. 'It's time to move on.'

'I have moved on.'

'So why are you living in that massive house on your own?'

Because he liked being on his own.

Mac opened his eyes and glanced at the mess. 'Last time I looked, you were living in it with me. And I wish you'd learn to clear up after yourself. This place is a pit.'

'You'll miss me when my boathouse is finished,' Josh said cheerfully, and Mac gave a ghost of a smile as he took a last glance around the kitchen.

'Will I?' He strode out of the kitchen and closed the door firmly behind him. The mess depressed him and he was too tired to tackle it. 'How are things there? Did you transfer the aorta guy to Theatre?'

'Don't change the subject. We were talking about you getting married again.'

'You were talking about that, not me,' Mac said irritably. Marriage definitely wasn't on his agenda. 'Did you get him to Theatre before it ruptured?'

Josh sighed. 'Yes, but you need to stop thinking about work. You need to ease off and develop different areas of your life. Achieve some balance.'

Mac frowned into the phone. 'Balance? Have you been reading women's magazines? And were you working in the A and E department with me last night or not? Did you happen to notice any drunk, abusive patients, brainless drivers and idiots who can't walk along an icy pavement without breaking a limb? Because they were all out in force. I'm knackered and I need my bed. I don't have time for balance and I don't have time for your psychobabble.'

'I'm not giving you psychobabble, I'm telling you where you're going wrong with your life.'

'That's why you called?' Mac eyed the mud on the hall floor and exhaled slowly. He was never in the house. How did it get so dirty? 'To tell me where I'm going wrong with my life? Thanks.'

'Actually, I called to arrange delivery of your

Christmas present. I've gone to a lot of effort. It's important that you're in.'

Mac checked his reflection in the hall mirror and grimaced. He looked like a bandit. He needed a shave and a sleep, although possibly not in that order. 'We never bother with Christmas presents.'

It was just one more thing to think about.

'Well, this year, we're bothering. Or, at least, I am.'

Mac sighed and made a mental note to buy something useless for his brother. 'All right, if you want to play Santa, we'll play Santa. But I hope my stocking is full of bottles.'

'Alcohol isn't the answer.'

'Surely that depends on the question.'

Josh chuckled. 'You're supposed to be a respectable doctor,' he reminded him sternly, his voice suddenly muffled as he broke off to issue some instructions to someone who was passing,

Mac eyed his reflection. 'I am a respectable doctor.'

Even if he didn't look like one.

'Well, just make sure you're in to answer the door because it can't be left on the doorstep.' There was a yawn in his brother's voice. 'I'll still be stuck here up to my armpits in broken bones and hacking coughs. I should have been a GP.'

'Then you would have seen a hundred patients a day with nothing wrong with them. Are you serious about this?' Mac shook his head in exasperation as he contemplated the possibilities. 'You've seriously bought me a Christmas present?'

'Yeah.' His brother's voice was a mocking drawl. 'It's the festive season, just in case you hadn't noticed. And knowing you, I'm sure you hadn't. To you, Christmas is just another day of work.'

'Fortunately for my patients.' Matt strolled through to his enormous living room. His enormous, empty living room. It was devoid of all evidence of Christmas. The long French windows faced the sea, providing him with a perfect view of wild surf, thrashed into a furious frenzy by winter winds and bitter cold. Most people preferred to sample the delights of the Cornish coast in the summer but he'd always preferred it in the winter. In the summer it belonged to the tourists, the hordes of visitors who arrived with buckets and spades and giggling children, covering the beach outside his back door. And then the weather cooled and they departed, leaving him to enjoy the best part of the year with other committed locals. To some it would have seemed stark and lonely but he loved the wildness. And he had no intention of adding tinsel just because it happened to be two weeks before Christmas. It was just something else to clear up.

'In case you've forgotten, this isn't exactly my favourite time of year.' He stared out at the ocean, realising that it had been weeks since he'd even found time to windsurf. Maybe his brother was right. Maybe he was working too hard.

'I know this isn't your best time of year, Mac.' His brother's voice softened slightly. 'But it's been two years since Melissa died and Santa's missed you. Get back on the horse, bro. It's time.'

Time for what?

Mac's fingers tightened on the phone. 'I appreciate

the thought.' His voice was rough. 'But I like my life the way it is.'

Busy.

'All you do is work, but my present is going to change all that. I've got to go.' Josh suddenly sounded harassed and Mac heard the sound of an ambulance siren and voices in the background. 'What's the matter with our department? The tourists have gone home and we're still inundated in A and E. We need to do some accident prevention work around here. Stop people driving too fast on narrow Cornish roads when it's icy.'

'It keeps us busy.' And he liked to be busy. Work was his life. Work was his saviour. 'What's happening about the nursing situation?'

'All sorted. She starts on Monday.'

Mac frowned. 'Who starts?'

'The new A and E nurse. She's a whiz. You'll love her. And now I've got to go. Lives to save. Nurses to impress. Talk to you later. Merry Christmas.' The phone went dead and Mac gave a sigh and replaced the handset.

He could just imagine what his brother was facing. They were so understaffed at the moment that the situation was becoming almost dangerous. As the consultant in charge of the department, he'd put his case to the hospital authorities on several occasions, but nothing had been done and the arguments were always the same. No more budget. And no staff willing to bury themselves in the depths of Cornwall, particularly in the winter.

Which meant that Christmas was going to be busy.

Exactly the way he liked it.

CHAPTER ONE

IT WAS her perfect house.

And there was no one home.

Louisa tried the doorbell again and cuddled her long wool coat around her to keep out the freezing wind. It had started snowing again and soft flakes settled on the ground and clung to her tumbling dark hair. She'd only stepped out of her car a few minutes before and already her fingers were freezing and she couldn't feel her toes.

If she was going to spend Christmas here, she needed more clothes.

She gave a shiver and pressed the bell again, this time keeping her finger on it for much longer. *Someone* had to be there. Josh had assured her that his brother would be at home. That he was expecting her.

Giving up on the bell, she took a step backwards and looked at the huge white house. It was gorgeous. The sort of house she'd dreamed about as a child. The sort of house that should have been full of kids and dogs and laughter. She stared, wistfully. On the ground floor, huge glass windows faced out to sea across a wide deck, piled with drifted snow. A large, rambling garden stretched all the way down to the sand dunes, wild and neglected.

It was a house with a story to tell. And today there were no signs of life.

Remembering everything that Josh had told her

about his brother and why he hated Christmas, Louisa stared anxiously at the house.

Just how much did Mac Sullivan hate Christmas?

Did he hate it enough to—to…?

She gazed up at the huge windows and bit her lip. Christmas was a bad time of year for lots of people, even without tragedy in their lives. What if he was lying in there, an empty bottle of tablets by the side of his bed? Maybe he'd left a note—

No.

She shook herself and wished her imagination wasn't quite so lively. He was probably just watching TV or something. He probably couldn't hear the doorbell.

Wishing she'd worn a thermal vest under her jumper, Louisa walked up to the window and peered inside, hoping to see signs of life.

She'd been told to arrive at lunchtime and this was lunchtime.

The living room was elegantly furnished with large white sofas set on a rich wooden floor, but the room had a formal feel that suggested that no one actually sat on the sofas. The cushions were plumped and smooth, like something prepared for a photographic shoot for an upmarket magazine.

It didn't look lived in.

She frowned thoughtfully. A house like this was meant to be a home and this didn't look like any home she'd ever imagined. Especially not at Christmas. A room like that should be filled with holly and presents and a massive tree.

Did Mac Sullivan have no one to buy presents for?

Had he shut everyone out since his wife had died?

Blowing on her fingers to warm them, Louisa gazed up at the upstairs windows but they were all firmly shut.

Worry started to gnaw at her brain again and she gave a shiver and mentally listed the options. She could stand still and wait for someone to turn up, but that could take for ever and would be of no help at all if he was really in trouble. Or she could give up on the whole idea and drive back to London, but that would mean being unemployed. And being on her own at Christmas. Not to mention letting Josh down when she'd promised she'd step in and help.

And, anyway, she couldn't possibly leave before she knew that Mac was all right.

Which meant finding another way into the house so that she could check that he wasn't lying in a heap somewhere.

Deciding that living in rural Cornwall meant being resourceful, she picked her way through the snow to the back of the house and immediately saw the open window.

Her eyes narrowed as she measured the space. Just large enough for her to wriggle through.

It had been a while since she'd used a window to gain access to a building but in this case it seemed like the only option. And she *was* expected so it could hardly be classed as breaking and entering, could it?

Mac heard the muffled thud the moment he switched off the shower. Someone was in the house.

He was being burgled.

Questioning the sense of tackling a burglar half-naked, he grabbed a towel from the heated rail and looped it round his hips before padding barefoot onto the landing to investigate.

There was another clatter and he winced. Whoever it was didn't have a great future as a burglar.

Probably someone who knew he was a doctor and thought he might keep drugs on the premises. Some crazed addict looking for a fix?

His dark hair was wet from the shower and he raked it out of his eyes with an impatient hand before reaching for a hammer that he'd used a few days before to put up a shelf.

His dark eyes gleamed with anticipation and he walked softly downstairs, his feet leaving damp marks on the carpet. As he reached the bottom, he wondered whether it was better to take the man by surprise or make a din and warn him of his presence.

In the end he went for the surprise option. Growing up with a brother, he'd never been afraid of the physical. He was six feet two and he had a black belt in judo. He was pretty confident that he could take most people, even dressed only in a towel.

The noise came from the visitors' toilet and Mac's mouth tightened as he recalled the number of occasions he'd asked Nicola, the last and most determined of his housekeepers, to sort out a lock for that window. It hadn't closed for months but it was one of the many things that she hadn't managed to fix before she'd walked out on him. Once he'd made it clear that he wasn't interested in a relationship it had appeared that she was no longer interested in working for him.

And his house was falling apart. He spent too long

at the hospital to do more than the most basic maintenance and this house needed far more than basic.

And now he was paying the price.

Shifting his weight to prepare for a fight, Mac pushed open the door to the toilet and pounced, his weight taking the other person down hard. 'Don't move!'

There was a shocked gasp from beneath him. 'How can I possibly move? You weigh a ton! And you're soaking wet!'

Registering a distinctly feminine voice, Mac gave a grunt and shifted his weight slightly, his hands grasping hers firmly and holding them above her head. He didn't intend to drop his guard just because his intruder was a woman.

He stared down into the widest, brownest eyes he'd ever seen and felt something stir inside him. She was soft and yielding under him and she smelt like a dream. Clouds of dark hair dusted with snow framed a perfect heart-shaped face and her soft cheeks were pink from the cold. *And she was laughing.*

'OK, muscle man—are you going to lie on top of me all day?' She sounded slightly breathless as she gazed up at him, her smile almost as wide as her face, 'because I ought to warn you that you're making it jolly hard for me to breathe.'

He rolled away from her, thinking that she looked nothing like a burglar.

She looked like something straight out of a bad boy's dream.

Reminding himself that he wasn't interested in becoming involved with a woman, especially one who had just wriggled through his toilet window, he frowned down at her.

'What the hell are you doing, climbing through my window? You were looking for a doctor?'

'Well, in a manner of speaking, I was looking for a doctor, yes.' She struggled to sit upright, her long legs going in different directions like a foal who still hadn't quite got the hang of standing. 'But I'm not a patient. Or at least I wasn't until you landed on top of me. Now I'm not so sure. I think there's a distinct possibility that I'm injured. Possibly seriously. Were you planning to use that hammer on me?'

'Only if you proved to be especially violent,' Mac said dryly, placing the hammer on the window-seat and holding out a hand to help her up. Her skirt had ridden up almost to her bottom and he found his attention snagged by her legs. *She had fabulous legs.* 'Do you always climb through windows when you're looking for a doctor?'

'Never before. But I was worried that you might be lying unconscious at the top of the stairs, unable to call for help. I thought you might need rescuing.' She reached out and took his hand and he pulled her to her feet, surprised to find that she wasn't as tall as he'd thought. Obviously most of her was leg.

He dragged his eyes away. 'Why on earth would you think that?'

'Because I rang the doorbell and no one answered.'

He lifted an eyebrow. 'And that meant I was lying unconscious? You didn't think I might be out buying a loaf of bread?'

'I have a vivid imagination,' she confided happily, her wide smile lighting up her whole face. Her eyes were the colour of rich coffee and a few freckles dusted her nose. 'There didn't appear to be a shop open in the village, so you couldn't have been buying bread.'

'So you thought you'd break in?' He stared at her with incredulity. 'Is that a frequent habit of yours?'

'Only when essential. It's part of my naturally interfering personality.' She brushed herself down and shook the snow out of her hair. 'I'm so relieved you're all right. So, if you weren't lying unconscious, why didn't you answer the door?'

His eyes narrowed as he looked at her. 'Because I was in the shower.'

'At lunchtime?'

Mac sighed, wondering why he was explaining himself to this woman. 'I was up all night in the unit. Motorbike accident. The roads are lethal at the moment. When I came in I spent ten minutes arguing with my brother and then got stuck into some paperwork before deciding to take a shower. Are there any more details of my life that you feel you need to know?'

She wrinkled her nose thoughtfully. 'Probably, but they can wait until later. The most pressing thing is to dry myself off and get settled in. Where do I put my things?'

Deciding that he must be more tired than he'd thought, Mac stared at her blankly. 'Put your things? What do you mean, put your things?'

She waved a hand towards the window. 'I left my bags in the car but the boot leaks terribly so I really ought to bring them in before they get damp. It's snowing again. But, of course, you know that because it's all over me.' As if to prove her point, she shook herself like a kitten and more snow drifted onto the floor. 'Let's look on the bright side. At least I didn't fall head first down your toilet. That would have been an unhappy experience.'

Mac studied her in silence, an uneasy suspicion forming in his mind. 'You haven't told me what exactly you're doing here...'

'No, I haven't, have I?' She smiled warmly and held out a hand. 'Your brother said I could come. I needed somewhere to stay and he told me you needed help. So here I am. Apparently I'm your Christmas present. Pleased to meet you, Dr Sullivan.'

Her new boss had a fantastic body and at the moment virtually every delicious inch of him was on display.

Louisa stood in the corner of the small room, trying not to focus on that broad chest or the well-defined muscles of his abdomen. If she'd needed the perfect illustration of the male anatomy then it was standing in front of her. His body was hard and tough with no soft edges. The body of a man used to strenuous physical activity.

And as for the rest of him...

With a huge effort of will she stared into his cold, handsome face and forced herself to breathe normally.

Josh had told her that the house was huge. He'd told her that the Cornish seaside fishing village was so small that you couldn't sneeze without the entire population asking you about your cold the next morning.

What he'd failed to mention was the fact that his brother was drop-dead gorgeous.

And angry.

His eyes glittered dangerously and there was no trace of amusement in his hard features.

'Is this some sort of joke?' His voice was suddenly icy cold and he was looking at her with all the enthusiasm of a pathologist looking at a deadly virus. 'How can you be my Christmas present?'

She tilted her head to one side. 'Because your brother arranged it. I'm Louisa.'

He closed his eyes and muttered something under his breath. It sounded suspiciously like, 'I'm going to kill him.'

Louisa stood for a moment, waiting patiently, and finally he opened his eyes and his gaze fixed on hers.

'All right, this is what we're going to do. We're going to rescue your things from your car before they're soaked, we're going to get you dried off and then we're going to sit down and talk about this. Because whatever you and my little brother have cooked up between you, it isn't going to work for me. Once you've had a hot drink and dried off, I'm sending you on your way.'

Louisa looked at him. 'Josh didn't tell you I was coming?'

He ran a hand through his hair in a gesture of pure exasperation. 'No. Well, yes, sort of. He told me he'd arranged my Christmas present. He just omitted to tell me what it was.'

Louisa covered her mouth with her hand and gurgled with laughter. 'That's so like Josh. He probably thought that if he told you in advance, you'd refuse to let me through the door.'

His black eyes were flint hard and as cold as the Arctic. 'He would have been right.'

Oops.

She smiled placidly, refusing to let him intimidate her. 'So it's just as well I came through the window, then.' She'd never met a man with more defences but she wasn't put off by his lack of warmth. Josh had warned her that his older brother would try and keep her at a distance and she had no intention of being sent away until she'd helped. And she *knew* she could. 'OK.' She glanced down at herself with a rueful smile. 'I'm dripping all over your floor. If you don't want me to catch a cold, you'd better show me where I can get dried off and changed.'

He studied her for a moment and then let out a sigh of undisguised exasperation. 'Upstairs, first on the right. There's a guest bedroom and bathroom. Use it and then you can be on your way. In the meantime, I'll get your things. Keys?'

He held out a hand and she looked at him blankly. 'Oh…' She smiled in sudden comprehension. 'I never lock my car. It's such a wreck no one in their right mind would ever want to steal it.'

She followed him into the hallway and stopped dead in the large hallway, her eyes fixed on the sweeping staircase. 'A fairy-tale staircase. I've never actually seen one in real life, only in films. That's amazing,' she said huskily, her gaze wistful as she gazed upwards. 'Just like the one in *Gone with the Wind*. You could sweep a woman off her feet and carry her up those stairs—'

'Or she could walk,' he said tightly, piercing her

dream with a sardonic lift of a dark eyebrow. 'I thought you were catching cold?'

Obviously not a romantic.

'I am.' She walked slowly up the stairs, trailing her hand lovingly up the oak banister. 'The wood is beautiful.'

'I restored it,' Mac said irritably, and she peeped at him quizzically.

'You know, you should probably get some sleep.'

'Why would I want to do that?'

'Because you look tired. You're also very, very crabby and that's always a sign of tiredness.'

His dark eyes burned into hers. 'It's also a sign that my brother has introduced a strange woman to my house when I don't need one.'

'Men are always hopeless at knowing what they need,' Louisa said sagely, 'but fortunately for them, women are here to help them work it out. Do you think you could rescue my bag from the boot before everything is soaked through?'

He was staring at her with an expression of stunned disbelief on his handsome face. 'Your bag...' His tone was almost faint. 'I'll get it.' He seemed to shake himself. 'And once you've dried off, you're leaving. I'm not blaming you and it isn't personal. I'm fully aware that none of this is your fault and I intend to take it up with my brother. Bedroom is second on the right.'

Ignoring the frost in his tone and the ice in his eyes, Louisa followed his instructions and pushed open the door. The place had been decorated like a traditional beach house. Floor-to-ceiling windows, scrubbed floorboards and a huge bed covered in white bedding and creamy throws. There were touches of blue, interesting pieces of driftwood and piles of shells stacked in pretty bowls. Even in the depths of winter the room seemed to feel summery and light. And she loved it. She gazed out of the window as Mac strode in with her bags.

'You were right. They're soaking wet. Put them near the radiator and they should dry off.' He dumped them on the floor and frowned at her. 'Is something wrong?'

Her eyes were still on the sea. 'Oh, no, nothing's wrong—' She broke off and cleared her throat. 'Everything is right. I just love it here.'

Her dream.

A house by the sea. A village where everyone knew each other. Surely in a place like this a person could *belong*.

'Well, don't get too settled. You won't be staying.' His frown deepened and there was a moment's silence, as if he regretted his rudeness. 'Most people hate the beach in the winter,' he said gruffly. 'They find it wild and lonely.'

Louisa thought of her early childhood spent in a cramped high-rise flat in the middle of a soulless city until Social Services had taken her away. 'I suppose loneliness means different things to different people.' She pulled herself together and turned to face him, a bright smile on her face. 'I'll take a shower and change, if that's all right with you, and then we can meet downstairs so that you can tell me again that this is all a mistake and I can't possibly stay.'

He paused for a moment, his dark eyes wary, and

then he gave a reluctant laugh. 'Why do I have a feeling you're going to be difficult to shift?'

Without waiting for an answer, he left the room and Louisa stared after him thoughtfully. 'Oh, I'm not going to be difficult to shift, Dr Mac Sullivan,' she muttered thoughtfully. 'I'm going to be impossible.'

He needed her.

She'd always been good at reading people. It was her special gift. And all her senses warned her that Mac Sullivan was a troubled man. She could feel the tension in him. Feel the way that he pushed people away. Shut himself off.

Josh was right about one thing, she mused as she unzipped her bag and pulled out a warm jumper. His brother was going to do everything in his power to get her to leave.

She cuddled the jumper and for a moment her eyes swung back to the sea. The winter wind whipped the waves into a foaming mass and the sky was grey and laden with the threat of more snow.

It was cruel and cold and unwelcoming.

So why did she feel she was finally home?

CHAPTER TWO

DOWNSTAIRS, Mac put the kettle on the Aga and called his brother. 'I owe you a black eye. Your Christmas present just arrived.'

His brother chuckled. 'Isn't she gorgeous? I've excelled myself, haven't I?'

Mac felt the irritation rise. 'When I need a pimp,' he said tightly, 'I'll ask for one.'

'Hey!' Josh's voice was suddenly sharp. 'Don't speak that way about Louisa. Believe it or not, this time I'm not fixing you up. This isn't about sex.'

Mac rolled his eyes as he waited for the water to heat. 'With you, everything is about sex and you've been trying to fix me up since the day Melissa died. And frankly I just don't need it. I don't need another woman in my life.'

He was no good at relationships.

He was better off on his own.

An image of Louisa with snow scattered through clouds of curling dark hair filled his brain and he pushed it away. It was all part of his brother's plan and he wasn't falling for it. He was perfectly satisfied with his life.

'This isn't just about you.' Josh sighed. 'Mac, we're drowning under work. We don't have time to turn around. We need someone to help in the house and we need another nurse in the department. Louisa fits both slots. She'll make all our lives easier. If you

24

frighten her off, I swear I'll kill you with my bare
hands.'

'She's the nurse you were talking about?' Momentarily preoccupied, Mac suddenly felt steam sear his
wrist and stepped back with a soft curse. Functioning
on automatic, he lifted the kettle off the heat and ran
his arm under the cold tap, his mouth set in a grim
line. 'I appreciate the sentiment, Josh, really I do.' He
increased the flow and frowned at the red streak appearing on his wrist. 'But I don't need my brother
arranging my love life.'

'No, what you need is to stop shutting people out,'
Josh said shortly, 'and that's why I've bought you
Louisa.'

'You've *bought* me Louisa?'

'I'm paying her salary for a month. After that it's
up to you. But Louisa is the nicest person I know. A
real giver. And on top of that she's a brilliant A and
E nurse. She's going to be the answer to our prayers,
bro, so stop complaining. It's just for Christmas.'

'If she's so wonderful, why aren't you sleeping
with her?'

'Truthfully?' Josh laughed. 'Because she wouldn't
have me. She's too wise. But she's one of my favourite people. Let her stick around and you'll see
why.'

Mac turned off the cold tap. 'I have no intention
of letting her stick around. If she wants to work in A
and E, that's great, heaven knows, we need the staff,
but she's not living here with us.'

He needed his space. He couldn't think of anything
worse than being closeted with someone over the

Christmas period. When he wasn't working he just wanted to be left on his own.

He wanted peace and quiet and his own company. He didn't want tinsel and forced jollity.

'Fine.' Josh's tone was cool. 'Then she'll be homeless but I dare say she can sleep in a hedge. It won't be the first time. I've got to go. Patients calling.'

Mac replaced the receiver and cursed under his breath. He was well aware that Josh was the reason he'd got his life back together after Melissa had died.

But, dammit, that didn't give him the right to interfere with every aspect of his life. He was doing OK, wasn't he? He didn't need any help. And he certainly didn't need to be given a woman as a Christmas present. Even if she was stunning, had impossibly long legs and smelt as good as a summer's day.

He closed his eyes briefly and then opened them to find her standing in the doorway, watching him, those coffee-brown eyes fixed on his face in silent question.

The shower had turned her cheeks pink and her dark hair hung down over her shoulders in a damp, curling mass.

She was astonishingly pretty and against his will his eyes slid to her soft mouth, noting that her lower lip was slightly fuller than her upper lip. In fact, he noticed a lot of things he would rather not have noticed.

Mac ran a hand over the back of his neck and gritted his teeth. 'I've been up half the night and I'm knackered. I don't need this right now…'

Her gaze slid over the kitchen, resting on the piles of unwashed plates, the mountains of cold, half-eaten food and the empty bottles. 'Looks to me as though this is exactly what you need,' she said softly, a sympathetic look in her eyes as she looked back at him. 'You know, when life gets tough, there's nothing wrong with asking for help. People should help each other. Particularly at Christmas.'

He closed his eyes. 'I don't need help.'

She waved a hand and glanced around her pointedly. 'Well, you need *something*, Dr Sullivan. Starting with a dressing for that burn. Do you have a first-aid kit?'

He looked down at the vicious red mark on his arm. 'It's nothing.'

'It's blistered.' She walked across to him and took his arm, moving it slightly so that she could take a better look. 'And if you don't dress it, the chances are it will get infected and then it will certainly be something. First-aid kit?'

He inhaled sharply and jerked his head. 'In that cupboard.'

Maybe if he let her dress his wound, she'd be satisfied and leave.

His eyes tracked her as she walked across the room, noting the swing of her hips and the grace of her movements. Then she reached up into the cupboard and he caught a glimpse of a perfect, rounded bottom hugged by snug jeans. Something long dormant sprang to life inside him.

'OK.' She delved in the cupboard and withdrew the right box. 'Let's hope there's something decent in here. Most of the doctors I know aren't great at putting together first-aid kits.'

She flipped it open, pulled out a few items and then walked towards him. 'Sit down.'

He tensed. 'I feel fine. I don't need to sit down.'

She put the first-aid kit on the table. 'But you're at least six-two and I'm just normal-sized,' she said patiently. 'If you stand up, it makes it harder for me. Sit.'

He sat, telling himself that he could at least assess her dressing technique.

She worked quickly, her fingers deft and gentle as she dealt with the burn and, for some inexplicable reason, her obvious skill irritated him.

He'd wanted her to be clumsy and inept so that he had an excuse to yell at her. But her touch was skilled and smooth, her movements economical and practised.

Cursing his brother, he sucked in a breath and pulled himself together. 'Look, I'm going to be blunt and if that offends you then I apologise.' He wondered which bit of her smelt so good. Was it her hair or her perfume? 'The department needs a nurse to cover the Christmas period but that's all we need. I don't know what my brother has said to you but I don't need anything more personal.'

Soft brown eyes lifted to his. 'Is that what you think this is? A set-up?' Her eyes danced with laughter as she covered the dressing with a bandage and secured it firmly. 'You think I have to pay for sex, Dr Sullivan? Do I look that desperate?'

Momentarily captivated by the thickness of her dark lashes, Mac felt a kick of pure lust in his groin. This girl undoubtedly had men dropping to their knees. He might have done so himself at one time had he not decided that it was all too complicated. Women wanted something that he wasn't capable of giving.

'I'm just saying I don't need a blind date,' he said tightly, and she laughed.

'I know you don't. But you need me. Look at the state of your kitchen.'

His gaze didn't flicker. 'I work twenty-two hours a day at the hospital.'

Her eyes softened with sympathy. 'I know, and it isn't good for you, but all that's going to change now I'm here. A lot of things are going to change, starting with the state of your house,' she said soothingly, closing the first-aid box and returning it to the cupboard. 'I can do all that, Dr Sullivan. When I'm not working in A and E I can make your life more comfortable. You've got me for a month. Make the most of me.'

'Are you seriously telling me you're prepared to clear up my kitchen?' Mac stood up and swayed. Damn. He was more tired than he'd thought. 'Whatever happened to equal rights? I didn't think women did things like that any more.'

She washed her hands and dried them. 'Well, I just happen to like creating a home. It's my hobby. And if I don't clean up your kitchen, we'll all die of something horrible so it's in my own interests. Don't worry. You'll be pulling your weight. You can carve the turkey, I'm hopeless with knives.' She frowned. 'You look shattered. When did you last sleep?'

Sleep? Mac closed his eyes and tried to remember. He gave up. 'Too long ago.'

'Then go,' she said calmly, giving him a little push.

'Forget everything and just sleep. We'll sort everything out when you wake up.'

Her smoky, gentle voice oozed over him, soothing his jarred emotions. He stared at her blankly, fatigue paralysing his normally sharp brain. 'You expect me to go to sleep and leave you here?'

'Dr Sullivan.' Her eyes twinkled like lights on a Christmas tree. 'I've never forced myself on a man yet and I don't intend to start now. Neither do I intend to steal the silver. Go to bed. And don't bother to lock your door. You're perfectly safe.'

He stared down into those chocolate brown eyes and felt something shift inside him.

And he knew he wasn't safe at all.

Louisa started in the kitchen.

Humming to herself, she filled three large bin bags with the rubbish and took them outside and then ran the dishwasher twice while she threw out piles of papers and scrubbed at the stubborn rings on the kitchen table.

Two hours later the surfaces and the floor were gleaming and the crockery was clean and neatly stacked away in the cupboards. Having checked the contents of the fridge and found them decidedly lacking, she was glad she'd had the foresight to stop at the supermarket on the way and stock up on emergency provisions.

She retrieved the bags from her little car and emptied them into the cupboards. Then she set about making supper.

Remembering the remains of the take-away on the kitchen table, she decided that her impromptu shopping trip had been inspired. She chopped, fried and stirred, filling the kitchen with delicious smells. Satisfied that the food would look after itself for a while, she took a last glance around the now gleaming kitchen, threw out some ancient newspapers and take-away menus and gave a nod.

'Much better. Now for the rest of the house.' She strolled out of the kitchen with the intention of being thoroughly nosy. For a man living on his own, Mac Sullivan had a big house.

She opened the door to the living room and blinked. It looked as though the room had never been used. 'Like something out of a magazine,' she observed to herself, closing the door again and walking back into the hall. Two more huge reception rooms, an elegant conservatory with views of the sea and the downstairs cloakroom that had been her route into the house.

Unlike the kitchen, the rest of the house was tidy. Unlived in.

She almost preferred the kitchen, she mused. At least it showed signs of life. The house felt cold and uninhabited. As if someone had given up hope.

Was that what had happened? she wondered.

Had Mac Sullivan given up hope when his wife had died?

She didn't know much about it, of course. Only the little that Josh had told her, that his older brother had lost his wife in a car accident two years earlier. *And that he'd done nothing but work ever since.*

Noticing the footprints on the hall floor, Louisa gave a sigh and wandered back into the kitchen to retrieve the mop.

Mac Sullivan might be a dedicated doctor but he definitely needed some help with the rest of his life.

Mac slept without moving for three hours and then woke to find that it was already dark.

He lay for a moment, listening to the winter wind howling around the house and trying to work out what was different, and then he remembered Louisa.

Cursing his interfering brother, he grabbed some clothes and made his way downstairs.

There was no way she was staying. He'd find her somewhere in the village. And he'd find her somewhere tonight. Before she had the chance to mess with his life.

Bracing himself for an unpleasant scene, he pushed open the kitchen door and stopped dead.

His brother Josh was convulsed with laughter, his feet up on the kitchen table—*the scrubbed, tidy kitchen table*—while Louisa stood in front of the Aga, talking non-stop and stirring something that smelt delicious. Her dark hair spilled down her back and her cheeks were flushed from the heat.

She looked extremely happy and totally at home.

'Hi.' She broke off in mid-sentence and threw a smile at him, still stirring. 'You slept well. Supper will be ready in five minutes if you're interested. If you're not then it will keep until later. I wasn't sure when you'd be hungry.'

Mac opened his mouth to tell her that she had to leave and then the smell hit him again. He wavered, caught in a battle between his stomach and his brain. His stomach won. He'd eat and then he'd tackle the subject.

'Fine.' He sprawled in the nearest chair, noticing that the floor was gleaming and the bin was empty. In fact, if it hadn't been in his house, he wouldn't have known it was his kitchen. 'It looks great in here,' he said stiffly. 'Thanks.'

'You're very welcome.' She removed the pan from the heat and reached for a wooden board. Her hands moved quickly, chopping, slicing and mixing, and then bowls started appearing on the table.

Mac watched with something close to fascination. He'd never actually watched a woman cook before. Melissa had been a career-woman so on the rare occasions that they'd been in at the same time to eat, they'd lived on fast food and take-aways. And his mother had always had help in the house.

Watching Louisa was like watching an artist at work.

Josh sniffed and gave a moan of pleasure as she placed a bowl of fluffy rice in front of him. 'I'm not the marrying type, but I swear to heaven I'd marry you if you'd have me, Louisa.'

'You're safe, Josh,' Louisa said soothingly, turning away to lift a casserole out of the Aga. 'I wouldn't have you in any shape or form. Given the contents of the take-away cartons, I gather you both like Indian food so I've made you curry, but hopefully mine is a tastier and healthier option.'

Mac glanced at the array of dishes and felt his taste buds spurt. 'You made curry?'

He was starving.

'That's right.' She went back to the oven and removed several more dishes. 'That's a lamb rogan josh and a chicken pasanda—very creamy with almonds.

Rice, naan bread, spinach with garlic and green beans. Enjoy.'

Deciding that difficult conversation could definitely wait, Mac helped himself, piling his plate with food and then turning his attention to his brother. 'So— what happened today?'

Without lifting his eyes from his plate, Josh reached for his beer. 'Usual story. Too many patients. Too few staff. Any chutney, Lu?'

Louisa pushed the dish towards him. 'It's fresh chutney. Tomatoes, red onion, coriander—try it. It's better for you than that sugary stuff you had hanging around in the fridge which, by the way, expired a year ago so I threw it out.'

Josh gave a sheepish smile. 'Oops.'

'The forecast is bad. It's going to be a difficult Christmas,' Mac said, forking lamb curry into his mouth. For a moment he sat still, savouring the flavour. A fabulous mix of spices exploded onto his palate and he just managed to stop himself groaning with pleasure. 'This is amazing.'

'Glad you like it.' Louisa helped herself to some chicken. 'Why are you so busy at work? Surely there aren't many tourists at this time of year?'

'Difficult to attract staff to deepest Cornwall,' Mac said, chewing slowly, his eyes fixed on her face. 'Which makes me wonder what you're doing here.'

Why would she agree to come and live with strangers at Christmas?

Josh choked on his beer. 'For crying out loud, Mac, finish the food before you insult the woman. If she deprives us of seconds, I'll kill you.'

Mac didn't smile, his eyes still on her face, searching for clues. *What exactly was she expecting from him?*

She held his gaze. 'I'm making your life easier, Dr Sullivan. That's what I'm doing here.'

He glanced round his kitchen. 'Housekeepers don't usually work out.'

'Because they keep hearing wedding bells.' Louisa's tone was placid and her eyes twinkled with humour. 'Josh told me. Don't worry, Mac, you're very good-looking but you're not my type.'

'So what's your type?' The question left his lips before he could stop himself, but she simply laughed.

'I haven't met him yet, but when I do, I'll let you know and I'll invite you to the wedding. More curry?'

Mac sat unresisting as she spooned the rich sauce onto his plate. 'Are all your meals as good as this one?'

'Well, if you'll let me stay, you'll find out,' she said cheerfully, a dimple appearing in her cheek. 'If you throw me out, you'll never know.'

It occurred to Mac that she smiled more than any woman he'd ever met.

But he was still going to ask her to leave. *As soon as he'd finished eating.*

'So you're an A and E nurse?'

'That's right.' She poured herself a glass of water. 'I left my last job a few weeks ago.'

'Why?'

Josh let out an exasperated sigh. 'For goodness' sake, Mac. You sound like the Spanish Inquisition.'

'Are you always this suspicious?' Louisa sipped her water and then put the glass down on the table. 'I'm a perfectly competent nurse, if that's what's worrying you. Your unit sister has my references if you want to check them.' She broke off and hesitated briefly. 'And I left because I didn't want to be in London on my own at Christmas.' She stood up and started stacking plates into the dishwasher. 'I always get restless at this time of year.'

Mac sat back in his chair. 'You don't like Christmas?'

'Oh, I love Christmas,' she said softly, closing the dishwasher with a click. 'It's my favourite time of year.'

He sensed that she was going to say something more and then her mouth closed firmly and she carried on clearing up. He watched as she busied herself around the kitchen and wondered what she was hiding.

Because he had a feeling she was hiding something.

He took a deep breath and prepared to question her further, and then he caught the warning gleam in his brother's blue eyes. 'All right. You can stay.' *What the hell was he saying?* 'Just for now. Once you start working in the department you'll find you won't have time to clean up after us.'

She'd get fed up and leave and that would save him the bother of sending her away.

The tension seemed to ooze out of her. 'I can stay? Really?' Her voice was husky and curled itself around his insides like velvet. 'Thank you.'

Josh grinned and put down his fork. 'Thank goodness for that. She would have been a pretty difficult Christmas present to send back.' He raised his glass and winked at Louisa. 'To a decent Christmas dinner for once in our lives.'

CHAPTER THREE

'SO MY Christmas present has so far tidied your house
and cooked you an amazing meal. And the coffee she
left for us this morning was the best I've tasted. Any
time you want to thank me, just go ahead.' Josh threw
a smug smile at his brother and held out his hand to
one of the A and E nurses, who was hovering with
some X-rays. 'Are those for me?' He took the X-rays,
flicked on the light box and whistled. 'Just look at
that.'

'I'm looking.' Mac narrowed his eyes. 'That's a
nasty fracture. Did you call the orthopods?'

'No, I thought I'd fix it myself in my lunch-break,'
Josh drawled sarcastically, a wry smile touching his
mouth as he glanced at his brother. 'Of course I called
them. What do you think I am, a first-year medical
student who you have to watch out for?'

'Sorry.' Mac gave an apologetic smile and ran a
hand over the back of his neck. 'You may be a consultant but to me you're still my kid brother.'

'The kid brother who works like a dog so that you
can get some sleep at night,' Josh reminded him,
yanking the X-ray out of the light box and returning
it to the brown envelope. 'I'd better go and talk to
the relatives. Have you seen Louisa this morning?
How's she getting on?'

'At first glance she seems good,' Mac conceded,
walking with his brother back through the department

towards the trolley bay. 'Certainly knows her way round an A and E department.'

'And she knows her way round a kitchen, too, which has got to be good. I'm sick of take-aways.' Josh gave a shudder and came to a halt outside one of the treatment rooms. 'Just don't frighten her off with any more of your sharp remarks. I'm looking forward to tasting proper turkey for the first time in years.'

Mac sighed. 'I want to make sure that she doesn't get any ideas. She was giving me ''I want to save you'' looks this morning.'

It happened all the time since Melissa had died and it drove him nuts.

'Has she thrown herself at you?'

'No, but—'

'Trust me.' Josh's tone was dry. 'Even you wouldn't get that lucky. Louisa doesn't do casual relationships.'

Mac looked at his brother, his hackles rising for some reason he couldn't fathom. 'You've tried?'

'Do I look stupid?' Josh threw him a wicked grin. 'Of course I tried. Several times, actually. She wouldn't have me.'

Mac hid his surprise. He knew only too well that most women found it hard to resist his younger brother. 'In that case, she's just gone up in my estimation.'

'Thanks.'

Mac shrugged. 'I still don't understand why she would want to come to Cornwall in the middle of winter to look after two strangers.'

'Speak for yourself. I'm not strange.' Josh smothered a yawn. 'And the answer to that will become clear once you get to know Louisa.'

Mac frowned. 'Meaning?'

'OK.' Josh took a deep breath, his blue eyes serious for once. 'Louisa doesn't like being on her own at Christmas. On top of that, she's a genuinely kind and generous person who can't pass someone in trouble without trying to help. Watch her in action and you'll see what I mean. She's a fixer.'

'So what exactly is she fixing with me?'

'Your life,' Josh said, slapping him hard between the shoulder blades, 'and, goodness knows, it needs it.'

'I know I've broken it, Nurse.'

Louisa stared down at the badly deformed wrist and then at the wrinkled, aged face of the lady looking at her so anxiously. 'I think you're right, Alice,' she said gently. 'I'll get a doctor to look at it and then we'll take some X-rays. Try not to worry. We'll get it sorted out.'

'I can't believe this has happened.' Alice's eyes filled with tears. 'I should never have gone out but I wanted to do some Christmas shopping. I don't want to miss the last posting date. Vera is useless at that sort of thing, you see. The shopping is my responsibility.'

'Who's Vera?' Louisa reached for an X-ray form and filled in all the necessary details.

'My sister. She relies on me for everything,' Alice fretted. 'I'm the organised one, you see. She's not very strong. I look after her.'

Louisa glanced at the date of birth on the notes and

calculated that Alice was eighty-six. 'You look after her?' She kept her tone level, careful not to betray surprise or concern.

'Ever since her husband died twenty years ago. We argue, of course.' Alice gave a weak smile. 'But generally we rub along very well together. I'm the active one.'

Louisa mentally filed that information. 'Do you have any help in the home?'

'We've never needed any,' Alice said proudly, clutching her handbag with her good hand. 'I shop and cook and Vera manages a bit of housework around the place. We're a good team. And if we get stuck then someone in the village will always help. That's the good thing about living in a small community. Everyone looks out for everyone.'

Louisa smiled. 'Well, you might need some help with the shopping and cooking with that wrist out of action.' She tucked her pen back in her pocket. 'I'm going to get a doctor to take a look at your wrist so that we can get you sorted out.'

'You need a doctor?' Mac's deep drawl came from right behind her and she felt her heart jump in her chest. She turned quickly, feeling colour touch her cheeks as she met his cool gaze. Whenever she laid eyes on him she found it difficult to breathe.

Which was ridiculous, because Mac Sullivan was not a man who encouraged the attentions of women, even though he clearly attracted them.

He was brooding, gorgeous and too remote for his own good, she decided. Why did he insist on keeping people at a distance? Resolving to peel away the layers until she revealed the man underneath, Louisa turned her attention back to her patient.

'Poor Alice had a bit of a fall,' she said huskily, giving the old lady with a reassuring smile. 'I've filled out the X-ray forms but she hasn't been seen yet.'

Mac pulled out a chair and sat down so that he was at eye level with his patient. 'Pavements icy out there today, Mrs Ford?'

'Yes, and you're probably thinking that it was stupid of me to go out,' Alice fretted, glancing helplessly at Louisa. 'I should have stayed indoors but I needed some last-minute presents. The annoying thing is that I didn't even get round to buying them.'

'Don't worry about the presents,' Mac said calmly, examining the wrist with gentle fingers. 'Are you tender here?' He moved his fingers. 'What about here?'

'No, not particularly.' Alice watched as he checked her pulses and finished his examination.

'All right. That's fine for now.' He reached for the X-ray form that Louisa had already started filling in and signed it. 'We'll check your X-rays and then take it from there.'

'I can't stay in hospital,' Alice said firmly. 'I've got my sister to look after. She can't manage without me.'

Mac frowned slightly and stood up. 'Let's see what the X-rays tell us and then we'll worry about that.' He looked at Louisa. 'Give me a shout when the films are back.'

She nodded and watched as he strolled away, the bright lights of the A and E department glinting off his dark hair, his shoulders impossibly broad.

He wasn't her type, she told herself firmly.

He might be shockingly handsome but he was re-mote and distant and not at all tactile.

When she finally fell in love, it was going to be with a real family man. Someone who wanted a noisy, crowded home, just as she did, with hordes of chil-dren and several dogs.

Not someone like Mac who was self-contained and kept himself apart from others.

Did he even like children? she wondered.

'We've all worried about him since his wife died,' Alice said wistfully. 'Such a tragedy. We've been longing for him to find someone else but he only has time for his work. After she died we all mucked in, you know—made him food, tried to get him out and about, but he wasn't having any of it. Spends time with his surfboard and that playboy brother of his with the wicked smile.' She made a clucking sound with her tongue. 'What a waste. He's such a hand-some boy.'

Louisa chuckled. 'He's the senior consultant and in his mid-thirties at a guess. I don't think he's a boy, Alice.'

As far as she was concerned, he was all man. Every delicious, intimidating inch of him.

'When you're ninety, he's a boy,' Alice said dryly. 'Now, shall we take that trip to X-Ray?'

Louisa smiled. 'Good idea. Let's get a closer look at those bones of yours.'

'Well, it's not displaced so she can just go to the fracture clinic and have a backslab,' Mac muttered, studying the X-rays carefully, his broad shoulders brushing against Louisa, who stood next to him.

This close he could smell her perfume and it played havoc with his senses. He wasn't even sure if it was perfume. It could have been shampoo or just Louisa. But whatever it was, she smelt amazing.

He sighed and closed his eyes briefly, reminding himself that he wasn't interested in women. Once or twice he'd tried to rekindle that part of himself after Melissa had died, but women always wanted more than he was willing or able to give. He wasn't interested in a relationship. He was better off on his own.

'I expect we ought to write to her GP. This sort of fracture is very common in women with osteoporosis. He ought to arrange a DEXA scan.' Louisa frowned at the light box, oblivious to his scrutiny. This close he noticed that her nose turned up slightly and was dusted with freckles. She never seemed to stop smiling. She turned to look at him. 'Don't you think?'

Didn't he think what?'

He searched his mind for the last thing she'd said. 'DEXA scan. Good idea. I'll write to the GP.'

'I gather she lives down the road from you.' Louisa handed him the notes and he took them, wondering what his response was supposed to be. 'With her sister.'

'That's right.'

'She told me she used to cook for you sometimes.'

Mac looked at her. 'The two of them kept checking up on me after my wife died. Every time I came home one of them would be on my doorstep with a cake or a casserole.'

She smiled. 'How kind.'

Mac inhaled sharply. 'I prefer my privacy.'

'That's what I heard.' There was a hint of reproach in her voice and he bit back an impatient remark.

'Living in a village comes with disadvantages, Louisa,' he said grimly as they walked back towards the treatment room. 'One of those is a total lack of privacy. Not everyone wants to be surrounded by people discussing their business all the time, and I'm one of them. I'm better off on my own.'

'Why?' Her gaze was clear and direct. 'What's wrong with knowing your neighbours, Dr Sullivan, and allowing them to know you?'

He sighed. Somehow she managed to make him feel in the wrong. Which was ridiculous, because he gave enough of himself to his patients. He had a right to privacy. 'In case it's escaped your notice, I have a busy job. I give everything I have to the hospital. I don't have time for anything else.'

She nodded slowly. 'That's what I thought. But what about you, Mac? Who gives to you?'

He frowned. 'I have everything I need.'

'Maybe you don't know what you need.' She took the X-rays from him. 'This is going to cause Alice a problem. She looks after her elderly sister. Does everything. Shopping and cooking. She can't do that with a broken wrist.'

Mac gave a brief nod, impressed that she'd discovered that so quickly. 'Good point. We'll give Social Services a ring. Get them some help.'

'I'm not sure that they're the sort to accept help easily. They're obviously very independent.'

'Well, if there's no family to step in, what's the

alternative?' Mac asked patiently, and Louisa chewed her lip thoughtfully.

'I don't know, but I'm working on it.'

'Don't tell me.' His tone was dry. 'Your interfering personality again?'

'Probably.'

She looked so worried that Mac gave a sigh. 'She's a sweet lady, I grant you, but it isn't our job to care for her until her bones heal.'

She lifted an eyebrow. 'That's a cop-out.'

He inhaled deeply. She was doing it again. Making him feel guilty. 'What do you expect me to do? Move in with all my patients?' His tone was testy but he couldn't help it. 'Our job is to patch them up, Louisa. Someone else has to sort out the other stuff.'

'But I don't believe the ''other stuff'', as you call it, can be so neatly separated,' Louisa said calmly, tucking the X-rays under her arm. 'A patient is so much more than just a broken wrist.'

Mac's eyes narrowed. 'You're too idealistic. This is the real world, Louisa. Too many patients, too few staff. If we mend the broken bones then we're doing well. We certainly don't have time to sort out the rest of people's lives.'

She gave him a smile designed to melt the heart of the most hardened cynic. 'You're working too hard, Dr Sullivan. You've developed tunnel vision. These patients of yours are human beings, not bones. And Alice is your neighbour.'

'You can drop the ''Dr Sullivan''. If you're going to abuse me, you may as well use my first name,' he said dryly, and she chuckled.

'All right, but I still think you're working too hard. Someone needs to reintroduce you to the world.'

'And you think that's you?'

She grinned, undeterred by his cool tone. 'Maybe.'

They walked back to Alice who looked at them anxiously. 'Well?'

'We're going to put that wrist in plaster,' Mac said briskly and Alice gave a gasp of horror.

'But it's Christmas! How will I cook?'

How the hell did he know? Mac stared at her, bemused and totally at a loss to know how to answer the question. Then Louisa intervened, slipping her arm round the old lady and giving her an impulsive hug.

'Don't worry, Alice,' she said firmly, 'we'll work something out. You're just down the road from us and we're having a massive turkey so there'll be plenty over. I'll cook it and Dr Sullivan here will drop it round to you both. A thank you for all the times you cooked for him.'

Mac felt his jaw drop.

Alice's face brightened. 'You two are living together? Oh, that's *lovely*.'

Mac spread his hands and stifled a sigh of exasperation. 'Mrs Ford—'

'Please, call me Alice, dear.'

Mac blinked. No one had ever called him dear before. 'Alice—' he tried again '—we are *not* living together.'

'At least, not in the biblical sense,' Louisa said cheerfully, giving Alice a saucy wink. 'I'm just doing his shopping and cooking and generally sorting out his house. Everything a wife would do with none of the perks.'

Mac closed his eyes.

'Well, that is good news.' Alice chuckled. 'I can't *wait* to tell Vera.'

Great. Now he was going to be the talk of the village once again. Just when he'd managed to get them off his back.

'I'm off duty in ten minutes,' Louisa was saying, 'and as soon as you've had your wrist plastered I'm going to take you home via the shops so that I can pick up those presents of yours. You can wait in the car. Do you have a list?'

Mac opened his eyes and stared at her in disbelief. It was one thing to worry about what happened when a patient was discharged, quite another to offer to cook her lunch and do her Christmas shopping. He ran long fingers through his dark hair. 'Louisa…'

She smiled at him, her brown eyes twinkling. 'Calm down, Dr Sullivan, or you might burst something important. I'll just take Alice to the fracture clinic and then I'll take her home. One of the perks of living in the same village.'

Alice gave a sniff. 'You're a kind girl,' she said gruffly, and Louisa shook her head.

'No, I'm just naturally interfering.' She gathered together the old lady's belongings and handed them to her. 'Hang onto these and don't forget to dig out that list. I might add a few things to it myself. I haven't even started my shopping yet. You can help me decide what I should be buying. And I probably ought to order a turkey while we're at it.'

* * *

Louisa arrived home two hours later to find the house still empty. Clearly Mac was still at the hospital. Didn't the guy ever come home?

She dropped six bulging carrier bags on the hall floor and set to work.

First she went through the pile of post she'd retrieved from his bin the day before. Then she rummaged about in the bags for the ribbon she'd found in the market and found herself a pair of scissors.

An hour later she'd fastened even lengths of red ribbon to the hall wall and carefully attached all the Christmas cards.

Once the cards were displayed, she wandered into the garden and attacked the holly bush. What was the point of having a house like this one if you didn't make the most of it? she reasoned, admiring the clusters of scarlet berries that nestled among the shiny green leaves.

She worked quickly, snipping and arranging, occasionally pausing to stand back and admire her handiwork. Finally she was satisfied.

And her stomach was rumbling.

When Mac walked in, hours later, he was hit by delicious smells wafting from the kitchen.

His stomach rumbled and he gritted his teeth.

It was all part of her ploy to persuade him to let her stay and interfere in his life. And he wasn't falling for it.

He'd already decided that she had to leave. And he'd found her a room in the nurses' home.

Closing the front door, he shrugged off his coat and stopped, his attention caught by the total transformation of his hallway. It had been plain magnolia when he'd left the house that morning. Now it was anything but plain.

Somehow she'd managed to bring the garden inside the house. Prickly bunches of holly were artfully arranged around the large mirror, long sticks of twisted willow had been teased into two tall glass vases and now sparkled with tiny lights. Rows of Christmas cards fastened to strips of red ribbon fell from the picture rail and candles flickered in the window recess, sending out a scent of cloves and lavender.

The doors to his sitting room had been opened and a fire burned merrily in the hearth, casting shadows across the room.

The effect was warm and cosy.

And Christmassy.

Something lodged in his throat and refused to budge. For a brief moment the cloak he'd drawn over his emotions slipped aside and he felt a shaft of pain stab through him.

This was somebody else's Christmas.

This wasn't what he did.

He gritted his teeth and shrugged his broad shoulders out of his wool coat just as Louisa strolled out of the kitchen.

'You're so late—you must be totally knackered.' Her dark hair had been scooped into a ponytail and her cheeks were pink. He assumed she'd been standing in front of the Aga again.

He looked at the glass she was holding out to him. 'What's this?'

She grinned. 'Alcohol. I thought I'd butter you up so that you don't shout at me for decorating your hall and throwing open your living room. It has such fabulous views across the beach, we should be using it. The tree should go in there. We could—'

'Louisa!' He interrupted her sharply, ignoring the glass. 'Louisa, I don't want a tree. I never bother with a tree.' He waved his hand around the hall. 'Or any of this. And I don't want a drink.'

'Go on—it will relax you.' She forced the glass into his hand. 'I go for chocolate myself after a hard day, but I know that's a girl thing so I thought you'd prefer wine.'

Left with no choice, he closed his fingers round the glass and looked back at his hall wall, staring at the Christmas cards neatly clipped to ribbon. 'Where did those come from?'

'Your bin. It was full of unopened cards. Don't you ever open your post?'

'Only the bills.' Deciding that maybe he did need a drink after all, he lifted the glass to his lips. 'I don't have time for anything else. I never hang cards up.'

'Why not?'

'Because it's just something else to clear up after Christmas,' he admitted wearily, and her gaze drifted to the wall, now covered in cards.

'Do you send any cards yourself?'

He gave a flicker of a smile. 'What do you think?'

'I think you're a man who shuts everyone out and thinks about nothing but his job,' she said softly. 'And it isn't good for you. Lots of those cards were full of kind messages—everyone is obviously worried about you.'

He tensed and sucked in a breath. 'I'm fine. And I'd rather people didn't worry about me. I certainly don't expect them to.' He caught her gaze. 'Why are you looking at me like that?'

It disturbed him.

'Because I don't think you're fine. I don't think you're fine at all, Dr Sullivan. I think you bury yourself in work because it stops you feeling or having to spend any time here, and when you eventually come home you're so exhausted you just drop into bed.'

'And what's wrong with that?'

'Because you're blocking life out instead of building a new one.'

'This is my life, Louisa,' he said coldly, 'and it's the one I want to live. Preferably without interference.'

She nodded, her eyes warm and gentle. 'I can understand why you feel that way. Josh told me about your wife. It must be difficult to pick yourself up again after that sort of loss. It's hard enough finding the right person once. How could you expect to do it twice?'

She had no idea…

Every muscle in his body tensed. It wasn't something that he intended to discuss with her.

'Are you always so direct?'

'Yes, usually.' She was unapologetic, her gaze clear and sympathetic. 'I think it's better to talk about the way you feel. But I suspect you don't agree. You don't like talking about your feelings, I can see that,' she said conversationally. 'Like most men, I suppose. You don't need to feel bad about it.'

Mac gritted his teeth. 'I don't feel bad about it. I just prefer to handle things my own way.'

'By burying yourself in your job.'

He stared at her in exasperation. 'Louisa, this isn't going to work.' He took a deep breath and dragged a hand over the back of his neck. 'I've found you a room in the nurses' home. You're a obviously a great nurse and I don't want to lose you, but I don't want you in my home.'

She went still and the colour drained from her face. 'The nurses' home?' She sounded so shocked that he found himself frowning defensively.

'There's nothing wrong with the nurses' home,' he said testily. 'It's a perfectly nice building. The rooms are great. You're looking at me as if I was suggesting you sleep rough.'

There was a look of horror on her pretty face. 'It's just that I'm not that great at institutional living. Especially not at Christmas.'

He sucked in a breath.

He wasn't going to feel guilty.

'It would be better for everyone.'

She shook her head. 'Not for me.' Shadows flickered across her eyes and for once there was no sign of her usually merry smile. 'I was hoping to spend Christmas in a house, with people.'

Mac clenched his fists.

He was *not* going to feel guilty.

'What about your own family?' He stared at her in exasperation, wondering why this was turning out to be so hard. 'Aren't they expecting you home for Christmas?'

He'd arrange for her to have the day off if that was what it took to get her out of his life.

There was a long silence and then she cleared her throat. 'I don't have any family, Mac.' Suddenly she sounded weary. Defeated. 'It's just me. Me on my own.'

He saw the loneliness shining out of her eyes and felt something twist inside him.

Damn.

He felt guilty.

'You must have someone. Everyone has someone.' He jabbed his fingers through his hair. 'Heaven knows, I have trouble getting rid of people. Every time I turn round I trip over someone checking if I'm all right.'

'That's because you live in a village where everyone looks out for their neighbours. You think they're nosy but I think they're caring. And I think you're lucky, Mac Sullivan. Lucky to be surrounded by people who give a damn how you're feeling and whether you're sad or not.' She gave a wistful smile. 'Weird, isn't it? You don't even know what you've got.'

Mac sighed. 'I like the village, I never said I didn't. But I also like privacy.' He eyed the decorations. 'And I don't do Christmas. It isn't my best time of year.'

'I know. Josh told me. And I'm sorry.' Her tone was flat. 'Maybe I got carried away, but I always do at Christmas. Everyone does family stuff and I don't have family. When Josh told me about the two of you on your own in this big house, I thought I could just move in and make it home for a few weeks. I wanted to do a fairy-tale Christmas. I thought you'd enjoy it, too. But perhaps I was wrong.'

Guilt throbbed like a vicious wound and Mac let out a breath.

'Are you saving me or yourself?'

She gave a brave smile. 'A bit of both?'

The bravery was his undoing. If she'd cried or begged he could have sent her on her way. But she didn't do either of those things. Instead, she managed to look strong and vulnerable at the same time, and the combination finished him.

He sighed. 'All right. You can stay.

Her look changed to one of cautious optimism. 'Really?'

He must be mad. 'Really.'

'Thank you.' She spoke with quiet dignity. 'I know I can make your life more comfortable and you won't even know I'm here.'

Oh, he'd know she was there.

One of the reasons he'd been determined to send her away was because he couldn't help noticing her. He noticed everything. The warmth in her eyes, the curve of her hips, the endless legs…

He stared into her soft brown eyes and felt something flicker to life inside him.

He really should send her away.

'Mac?'

He closed his eyes briefly. 'Just don't think you can rope me in on this fantasy Christmas that you're planning.'

'All right.' She chewed her lip and glanced around the hallway. 'But can the decorations stay and can we have a tree?'

'You're pushing your luck.'

She waved a hand around her hallway. 'It's just that your house is so perfect.' Her cheeks dimpled. 'A tiny tree? Just a few bits from the garden?'

His gaze flickered to the bursts of greenery that

now adorned his hallway. 'You've already transferred half the garden to the hall. I don't do Christmas, Louisa. But if you want to, that's fine with me.'

'Correction,' she said happily. 'You haven't done Christmas up until now. But this year you're doing Christmas, Mac. And you're doing it in style.'

He was more prickly than his holly, she mused as she tasted the casserole and added a pinch more salt and pepper.

After their encounter in the hallway, he'd disappeared upstairs and she wondered whether she'd see him again that evening.

Maybe she'd be eating the casserole on her own.

But at least he was letting her stay.

Ridiculously happy, she tasted the casserole again and then nearly dropped the spoon as she glanced up and saw him in the doorway, watching her.

He'd changed into a soft black jumper and a pair of black jeans which were moulded perfectly to his hard thighs. His hair was still damp from the shower and his eyes were flinty black. He looked disturbingly male and more sexy than any man had a right to be.

And he wasn't the right man for her, she reminded herself hastily, dropping the spoon into the sink.

He strolled into the room. 'Tell me how you met Josh.'

'Through work.' She dragged her eyes away from the dark shadow of his jaw and lifted the casserole onto the table. 'We met on an A and E course a few years ago.'

'And?'

'And he tried to get me into bed.'

Mac gave a short laugh and sat down. 'Sounds like my baby brother.'

'He didn't succeed.'

'Then he must be slipping.'

'No. He just isn't my type.' She mashed potatoes and added milk and butter until they were fluffy. 'He's terrified of commitment and he'll stay that way until he meets the right woman. And that woman certainly isn't me.'

'But he invited you here.'

She put the mashed potatoes on the table. 'Josh has got a heart of gold. He's worried about you and he's worried about me. He knew I had nowhere else to go.' She hesitated, wondering how much to tell him. 'And he knows I hate being on my own at Christmas.' She could feel his eyes fixed on her face.

'Christmas has a lot to answer for,' he said grimly, sitting back as she spooned casserole onto a plate. 'The media perpetrate this image of perfect families gathered round a twinkling tree loaded with presents. Faced with that fantasy, people can only be disappointed. It's no wonder the suicide rate is so shockingly high at this time of year.'

'Yes, other people's happiness has a way of driving you over the edge.'

His eyes narrowed as he took the plate from her. 'Astute, aren't you?'

'Well, I know all about being on the outside, looking in.' She pushed the potatoes towards him. 'Help yourself. What was Christmas like when you were young? I love hearing about other people's Christmases. Did you do the whole family thing, Mac?'

Somehow she couldn't imagine him as a child. Carefree. Laughing. Ripping paper off presents in a frantic haste to get to what was inside.

Mac seemed too serious for all that. Adult.

'Christmas.' He gave a brief shrug and started to eat. 'Turkey. Tree. Presents.'

She gave him a wistful look. 'Did you play games?'

'No, definitely not.' He shook his head. 'My parents entertained in lavish style. We usually had about thirty people for lunch. All Josh and I wanted to do was open presents and play, but we had to be on our best behaviour and sit for ages over the various courses that my mother produced.'

She pulled a face. 'That doesn't sound much fun.'

'I'm guessing it was better than yours,' he said softly, his eyes fixed on her face. 'Was yours very bleak?'

Oh, yes.

She toyed with her food. 'It was different every year.' She fought to keep her voice casual. 'A couple of times I was in foster-care over Christmas and that was all right—except that I never really felt part of the family. I was always the outsider.'

'And when you weren't in foster-care?'

'Different places.' She was aware of his gaze resting on her face and shifted uncomfortably. She had a feeling that Mac Sullivan didn't miss much.

'What happened to your parents?'

'My mother had me when she was sixteen and couldn't cope with me. I had asthma as a child and I used to be pretty ill, in and out of hospital all the time. I was shifted from foster-home to foster-home while they tried to find someone who'd adopt me, but people were put off by the severity of my illness.' She shrugged. 'I didn't fit people's image of a perfect baby, I suppose. I'm not maudlin about it. It's just the way it was. I got on with it.'

'But you hang onto this fantasy of a perfect family Christmas.'

He definitely didn't miss much.

'Now who is being astute?' She smiled. 'I'm not a victim, Mac. There are a lot of things I didn't have when I was a child, but I intend to make sure that I have them in the future.'

He reached for his glass. 'Like what?'

'A proper home. A man who loves me. A dog and several children.' Her cheeks dimpled into a smile. 'Probably five, actually.'

'Five?' He sounded shocked and she laughed.

'Yes. I want a noisy, crazy house where you can't have a moment's peace but where everyone is there for everyone else.' She bit her lip and gave a shrug. 'I want every Christmas to be the one I never had. I suppose I want the fairy-tale.'

'One person's fairy-tale is another's nightmare.' He gave a short laugh and helped himself to more casserole. 'This is delicious, by the way. You're an excellent cook.'

'I love cooking.'

He looked at her. 'You love playing house.' His tone was soft and she didn't even bother denying what was so obviously the truth.

'So now you understand what makes me tick, what about you? Did your wife cook, Mac?'

Had his wife played house?

His fork stilled. 'Is this part of your rehabilitation programme?' His voice was suddenly harsh. 'Get me to talk about Melissa?'

He could be formidable when he wanted to be, Louisa mused. No wonder he succeeded in keeping people at a distance.

'Pretty name,' she said quietly, 'and, no, it isn't part of any programme. Just a natural question as part of the conversation. Or doesn't she come up in conversation?'

He inhaled deeply. 'I don't want to talk about her, Louisa.'

His shoulders had gone from relaxed to rigid. If she'd been sensible she would have dropped the subject. But when it came to someone hurting, she wasn't always sensible.

'And does that help? Not talking about her?'

His gaze lifted to hers. 'Nothing helps.' He dropped his fork onto his empty plate and rose to his feet. 'Thanks for dinner.' And with that he left the room without a backward glance.

CHAPTER FOUR

'RTA COMING in, Mac,' Josh said, dropping the ambulance hotline. 'Car came off the coast road and went over the cliff. The driver has been trapped for two hours but they've just got him out and they're bringing him here now.'

Louisa stared. 'He went over the cliff and he's still alive?'

Josh shrugged. 'It's the right time of year for miracles.'

Mac rolled his eyes. 'Let's hope so. OK, folks, everyone into Resus. Let's move.'

They donned protective clothing while Mac, as team leader, briefed them on their roles.

'Louisa, you're airway nurse. Work with Josh. All communication with the patient to go through Louisa.' He barked out instructions as he dragged on gloves and eye protection. 'Circulation team—if that car went over the cliff, the chances are he will have glass and debris in his clothing so I want you wearing thick gloves to undress him.'

The radiographer hurried in and Mac glanced in her direction. 'Sue, I'll need standard X-ray films—chest, pelvis and lateral cervical spine.'

The radiographer nodded and started preparing the machine just as the doors to Resus swung open and the paramedics hurried in with the stretcher.

'This is Tim Norton, fifty-five-year-old man from Plymouth—lost control of the car on the ice.'

Together they transferred the patient from the stretcher to the trolley, carefully checking that the lines and leads didn't become disconnected or snagged.

As airway doctor, Josh was responsible for clearing and securing the airway and he quickly ran through the necessary checks. 'He's apnoeic. We need to intubate him. Louisa?'

He held out his hand and Louisa immediately passed him the laryngoscope and endotracheal tube, anticipating his needs.

'Tim, we're just going to put a tube into your mouth to help you breathe,' she said, speaking clearly in case the patient could hear her. She knew how important it was to give reassurance and explain everything that they were doing. 'You're in hospital now and we'll soon have you feeling more comfortable.'

Once the airway had been cleaned and secured, they turned their attention to Tim's cervical spine while the other members of the team quickly removed his clothing.

Mac stepped forward, examining both sides of the chest for bruising, abrasions and other trauma. 'Rapid, shallow breathing,' he muttered. 'Flail chest?'

Josh finished helping Louisa apply the spinal support. 'Paradoxical breathing?'

'Only if the segment is large, central or if the patient is fatigued.' Mac frowned, listening to the patient's chest carefully. 'He's got a haemothorax. We need to insert a chest drain and he needs a blood transfusion. Fiona—did you get those lines in?'

He was slick and smooth, totally in control of the situation as he carefully monitored what each individual was doing.

What an amazing doctor, Louisa thought to herself as she continued to talk quietly to the patient, offering reassurance and comfort even though there was no response.

She'd worked in several different A and E departments over the past two years and had encountered a variety of different doctors. Some fumbled, some panicked. Mac did neither.

The drain was inserted into the chest with the minimum of fuss and the blood arrived from transfusion and was duly warmed before being attached to the giving set.

'His vital signs aren't improving,' Josh muttered, and Mac nodded, his expression grim as he checked the patient's obs.

'Which means that either the shock isn't caused by hypovolaemia or that the patient is bleeding faster than we can replace it. My money is on the latter. Are the surgeons on their way?'

'Right here.' Phil Douglas stepped up to the trolley, his eyes on the patient. 'What have you got for me?'

'He's fractured ribs 5 to 11 and he's showing all the signs of an intra-abdominal bleed,' Mac told him, outlining the situation in a clear, concise fashion while Phil listened.

'Haemodynamically stable?'

They continued to talk and examine the patient and finally Phil gave a nod.

'All right, if he's stable enough let's get him straight to Theatre.'

Mac frowned. 'Are there any relatives?'

One of the nurses nodded. 'We're contacting them now.'

Mac looked up. 'Your patient, Phil.'

Phil rolled his eyes. 'And a merry Christmas to you, too.'

'Phew, I'm exhausted.' Louisa surveyed the mess in Resus and gave a sigh.

'Go home.' Hannah, the A and E staff nurse who had acted as circulation nurse, gave her a smile. 'You've been on since the crack of dawn. You deserve a rest.'

'I'll help you first. The last thing we need is another accident in here before we've restocked.' Like all A and E staff, Louisa understood the importance of keeping Resus ready for the next emergency. 'It will be faster if we do it together.'

And she liked Hannah. The pretty blonde girl always had a ready smile and was a hard worker.

'Well, if you're sure, thanks. Poor man. What a thing to happen just before Christmas.' Hannah tipped the debris from the intubation tray into the bin. 'I hope they make contact with his relatives soon. Someone out there must be worrying themselves sick about him.'

Louisa felt pain shaft through her.

'Not everyone has someone to worry about them,' she said casually. 'Perhaps he doesn't have any family.'

Hannah looked at her. 'You think he might have driven his car off the cliff on purpose?'

'I didn't say that.' Louisa brushed her dark hair away from her face and gave a weary smile. 'Let's hope not.'

'Well, Christmas does weird things to people,' Hannah agreed, running through saline and dextrose and hanging them ready from the drip stand. 'I'm not exactly looking forward to it myself.'

Louisa glanced up from the drugs she was checking. 'Are you working?'

'Christmas Eve, Christmas Day and Boxing Day,' Hannah said cheerfully. 'Never mind. I'll just have to hope that Santa drops Mr Right down my chimney to distract me.'

Louisa smiled. 'Anyone particular in mind?'

'Well, I wouldn't object to finding Mac Sullivan in my stocking,' Hannah quipped. 'But seeing as he's on everyone's Christmas list, I'm not holding my breath.'

'What about Josh?'

Hannah gave a womanly smile. 'I'd prefer to keep my heart intact, and falling for Josh would be a big mistake. He's gorgeous, of course, but too much the playboy for my taste.' She shrugged. 'Mac's different. Solid. Tough. You just know that when he eventually takes the plunge and falls for a woman again, it's going to be serious.'

Would he fall for someone again? Louisa mused as she snapped open a laryngoscope to check that the bulb was working. Or would he keep himself locked away for ever?

Not her type, she reminded herself firmly as she finished restocking Resus.

'All done.' Hannah glanced round the room and gave a satisfied nod. 'Go home. You look exhausted.'

She was exhausted.

The doors swung open again and Mac strode in. 'Child with severe asthma coming in—is this place ready?'

Louisa froze.

Of all the cases she dealt with in A and E, asthma gave her the most problems.

'Louisa?' Mac's tone was sharp and she jumped.

'Everything's fine,' she said quickly, licking dry lips and moving towards the intubation tray. *She could do this.* Quickly she snapped open the paediatric laryngoscope. 'How old?'

'Little girl, aged six. Hannah, can you meet the ambulance?' His voice was rock steady and he waited for the other nurse to leave the room before walking over to Louisa. 'Are you all right?'

'I'm fine.'

His eyes rested on her. 'Louisa, you're shaking.'

She swallowed. There was no fooling him. On the other hand, he *was* a doctor, and a skilled one at that. 'I'm not that great with asthma attacks—sort of takes me back to my youth. I remember how scary they are.'

He nodded and something flickered in his dark gaze. Sympathy? 'Hannah can deal with it. You're supposed to be off duty now anyway. Go home.'

'No.' She shook her head and managed a smile. 'I'll be fine. Honestly. I always am.'

His eyes held hers and tension hummed between them, a living, breathing force.

Louisa felt her mouth dry and her heart thud against her chest. He wasn't her type, she reminded herself weakly, and she'd never been one just to go for looks.

She looked away quickly and tried to concentrate on work. Her eyes scanned the drugs, anticipating what they'd need. Aware that Mac was still watching her, she worked swiftly, laying out various pieces of equipment in logical order. Then the doors flew open again and the paramedics hurried in with the little girl.

Louisa braced herself.

'This is Martha, aged six.' The paramedic handed over quickly, explaining what had happened and what drugs had been given. 'She was at the pantomime with her grandma.'

Mac stepped forward. 'And where's Grandma now?'

'At Reception, giving details.'

Louisa took one look at the child and felt her heart twist. The little girl looked exhausted, her skin pale and her eyes hollowed from the effort of breathing. 'Her respirations are 52,' she said crisply, reaching for the nebuliser, 'and her pulse is 150. Martha, sweetheart.' Her voice softened as she stroked the child's head gently. 'You're in hospital now and we're going to help you breathe. You're going to be fine.'

Please, let her be fine.

'Let's give her high-flow oxygen,' Mac instructed, his dark head bent as he examined the little girl, 'salbutamol via the nebuliser and some prednisolone. Is she taking theophyllines?'

The paramedic nodded and Mac glanced at Josh who had just walked into the room. 'She's very cyanosed, she's exhausted and her peak flow is less than a third of what it should be. Can you get me a paediatrician and an anaesthetist?'

At that moment Martha clutched at his sleeve, panic in her eyes as she struggled to breathe.

Mac gave her his full attention, his eyes locked on hers as he adjusted the mask. 'I want you to stay calm, angel,' he said quietly, 'and trust me. We're going to help you breathe, I promise. You're in hospital and you're safe. How was that pantomime? Was it good? Did you see the ugly sisters?'

Louisa felt herself begin to relax. There wasn't a hint of panic or urgency about him. Instead, he was calm and totally in control of the situation, his movements smooth and apparently unhurried as he worked. Even though she knew the child was dangerously ill, she felt a rush of confidence. If anyone could help the little girl, Mac could.

He continued to talk to the little girl, explaining what he was doing. Louisa handed him an IV tray and watched while he examined the little girl's arm for a vein.

'Paeds and anaesthetist on their way,' Josh said as he walked back into the room just as Mac slid the cannula into a vein.

'I need her weight—I want to give her a maintenance dose of aminophylline. Will you do the calculation? Grandma is outside somewhere—let's get her in here.'

Josh disappeared again and reappeared almost instantly with a piece of paper in his hand. 'Grandma's on her way. I've got the weight—have you got a vein?'

'Of course.' Mac secured the cannula and glanced at Louisa. 'OK, let's give her 100 milligrams hydrocortisone and add some ipratropium to the nebuliser. How are her sats?'

Louisa checked the reading. 'Coming up. Ninety-four per cent.' She handed him the various syringes with the ampoules to check.

'All right, folks, we need to maintain her sats above 92 per cent and we need to repeat her peak flow.'

Hannah came into the room accompanied by an elderly lady in a thick coat, clutching a handbag. She stared at the little girl anxiously. 'Martha?'

The little girl wriggled on the trolley and Mac put out a hand to soothe her. 'You're all right, sweetheart,' he said gruffly, 'Grandma's here now and she's going to give you a cuddle in just a minute. You're a brave girl. Is it easier to breathe now?'

Martha nodded and he gave her a smile that made Louisa catch her breath.

How could she ever have thought he wouldn't make a good father?

Something warm slithered through her veins as she watched him with the child. He was so strong. Dependable. And he'd be the *perfect* father.

Coping with that sudden revelation, she met his questioning gaze and felt herself colour.

Oh, help.

She'd told him he wasn't her type.

What would he say if she confessed that she'd discovered that he was *exactly* her type?

The anaesthetist and the paediatrician arrived together and there was another flurry of activity.

'She seems stable,' Mac said quietly, his eyes on the child's chest, 'but she's obviously going to need admitting.'

'We'll get her to the ward,' the paediatrician said, and they made the necessary arrangements to transfer the child.

'Obviously not a great pantomime,' Josh drawled, humour in his eyes now that the emergency had passed. 'Remind me to give it a miss.'

Hannah accompanied the child to the ward and ten minutes later Louisa found herself alone with Mac.

'You did well.' His voice was gruff. 'Do you still suffer from asthma?'

She shook her head. 'No. I grew out of it.'

'But you suffered badly?'

'Oh, yes.' Memories clouded her brain. 'I can still remember how scary it is not to be able to breathe. You were good with her. You calmed her down.'

He shrugged. 'We were lucky.'

'You were amazing.'

His dark gaze fixed on her and the tension built between them. Suddenly she was aware of every male inch of him. The broad, muscular shoulders, the powerful legs, the strong column of his throat. And his mouth. Her eyes drifted from his and rested on the firm lines of his mouth. What would it feel like to be kissed by Mac?

Without realising what she was doing, she swayed towards him and heard his sharp intake of breath.

'Louisa…' His tone was suddenly harsh and she gave a start and looked up at him.

'I—'

'It's time to go home. You're off duty.' His gaze was hooded, his expression revealing nothing of his thoughts.

He was icily remote once more and she took a step backwards, suddenly flustered.

She didn't usually react to men like this. She just wasn't interested.

But Mac was different to every other man she'd ever met.

Suddenly realising just how tired and confused she was, Louisa gave him a brief smile. 'Off duty. Sounds good. See you later.'

She picked up her coat and her keys and strolled towards her car, wondering why her legs ached so badly. She'd obviously spent too long on her feet. She slid inside with a sigh of relief and turned the key in the ignition. Nothing happened.

'No!' She thumped her palm on the wheel in frustration. 'Don't do this to me.' She turned the key again and pumped the accelerator, but the little car was totally dead.

She tipped her head back against the seat and closed her eyes, too tired to think of an immediate solution to the problem.

The driver's door was jerked open. 'What's wrong?'

She knew it was Mac without even opening her eyes. 'My car doesn't like cold weather.'

'Your car doesn't seem to like any weather. Are you planning to spend the night here?' His tone was dry and she smiled without bothering to open her eyes.

'Dr Sullivan, I'm too tired to care where I spend the night so this is as good a place as any.'

'That bad?' His voice softened and he reached into the car and removed her keys from the ignition. 'Come on. I'll give you a lift and we'll sort this wreck of yours out tomorrow. At least it isn't blocking anyone.'

She shook her head. 'I can't move.'

'That's what happens when you try and cook, clean and work full time,' Mac muttered, retrieving her bag and coat and throwing them in the back of his car. 'Now you know why Josh and I resort to take-aways. Something has got to give.'

'Yes, well in this case it's my legs,' she groaned. Her eyes opened and clashed with his and she felt her heart miss a beat. His jaw was dark with stubble, his eyes were tired and he was still without doubt the most shockingly handsome man she'd ever laid eyes on.

He lifted an eyebrow questioningly. 'In case you hadn't noticed, it's snowing again and I'm freezing to death here. Are you going to get into my car or am I going to have to carry you?'

She got out of the car and gave a squeal of shock as her legs slid from under her. 'It's icy!'

With a soft curse Mac caught her hard against him and for a moment she clung to him like a child, feeling rock-solid muscle under her fingers. Then she started to giggle.

'I didn't realise it was that slippery.'

'Louisa.' His voice was patient. 'For heaven's sake, stand up.'

Her feet slithered on the ice as she struggled to regain her footing, and he cursed again and braced himself as she almost took the two of them down hard.

'It's like an ice rink.' She was clutching at him and she couldn't stop laughing, and when she looked into his face she saw an answering gleam in his eyes.

'My car is all of three feet away.' His teeth were gritted as he braced himself to keep them both upright. 'Do you reckon we can make it?'

She was still clinging to him, although how he was managing to keep his footing she didn't know.

'Yes. OK.' She took a deep breath and gingerly released her grip on his arms. 'I can do this. I'm just not that great on ice.'

'I'd noticed. The trick is to walk purposefully.'

'Walk purposefully. I can do that.' She straightened, took one step and immediately landed hard on her bottom. 'Ow-w!'

'You're a disaster!'

'You told me to walk purposefully!'

Without further comment he scooped her up and deposited her in the passenger seat of his car before climbing in next to her. 'Are you hurt?'

She was laughing so hard she couldn't tell. 'I think I may have broken my bottom.'

He grinned in response, started the engine and then glanced towards her. 'Why are you staring at me?'

Because he was every woman's fantasy?

'Because that's the first time I've seen you laugh,'

she said, 'and it suits you. You should do it more often.'

'If you keep on falling on the ice, I probably will,' he said dryly, reversing out of his parking space. 'Don't think I'm some sort of sad figure, Louisa. I'm perfectly happy with my life.'

'That's because you don't know what you're missing.' She pulled a face and shifted in her seat. 'I think I've seriously broken something.'

'You want me to examine you?'

'I've got a feeling that's an offer I should refuse.' She winced as she tried to find a more comfortable position on the seat. 'Next time I step out of the car, remind me to wear crampons.'

'The roads are terrible,' Mac muttered, flicking on his windscreen wipers to try and clear the snow from the windscreen. 'Let's hope everyone has the sense to stay indoors.'

Louisa stared ahead, watching the snowflakes racing towards them out of the darkness, relieved that he was the one who was driving.

They turned onto the coast road that led to his house and Louisa squinted in front of her. 'Mac, stop!'

With a soft curse he gently pumped the brakes and pulled the car over. 'Now what?'

'Back there on the side of the road…' She twisted in her seat and tried to look out of the rear window. 'I saw something. A bundle.'

Mac ran a hand over his face. 'I didn't see anything.'

'Well, I think I did.' She fumbled with the doorhandle and he reached across and stopped her.

'Are you forgetting what happened last time you set foot on the ice?'

She didn't smile. 'I saw something, Mac, I know I did.'

He sighed and reached into the glove compartment for a torch before hitting his hazard warning lights. 'All right. Let's take a look.'

She opened the car door and flinched as snow swirled into her face, obscuring her vision. She slithered her way back down the road and then grabbed Mac's arm. 'There. Shine the torch there.'

He swung the beam in an arc. 'Nothing.'

She grabbed the torch from him and shone it slowly over the ditch. 'Mac! There! Something's alive.' She flung the torch at him and scrambled down into the ditch without thinking.

'Louisa wait.' Mac's tone was harsh and he caught her arm. 'You're going to hurt yourself!'

'But it's an animal.' She jerked her arm away and slid down into the ditch, gasping with shock as her feet slid through the ice and into a foot of freezing water. Floundering, she reached forward and grabbed the bundle, astonished by the weight. It was bigger than she'd thought. 'Mac, it's a dog. And it's injured. Can you take it from me?'

'Do I have a choice?' But he leaned forward and gently took the shivering dog from her arms, allowing her to scramble out of the ditch.

The snow was falling thickly now and she brushed the flakes away from her face with her sleeve. 'Quick, we need to get it back to your car so that we can see what's going on.'

'You're planning to put this soaked, muddy, wriggling wreck in my car?'

Frantic with worry, Louisa slipped off her coat and covered the dog. 'Oh, the poor little thing! Do something, Mac.'

'Are you always this impulsive? I'm a doctor, not a vet, and you're going to freeze without a coat. For goodness' sake, Louisa! Put it back on!'

She ignored the exasperation in his tone. 'He needs it more than me. All right, where's the nearest vet?'

Mac sighed. 'Back the way we just came. But I think that might be too far for this dog.' His tone gentled. 'He's on his last legs.'

Her eyes were huge. 'Then we'd better move quickly. We can't let him die. He must have been hit by a car and abandoned. Some child must be out there, pining for her missing pet.'

His eyes met hers. 'I hate to shatter your illusions but this dog doesn't look like anyone's much-loved pet,' he said gruffly. 'You have a vivid imagination.'

She sensed him weakening. 'But you'll take him to the vet...'

He rolled his eyes. 'Yes. But if he makes a mess of my car, you're cleaning it.'

'He's half-starved and bruised but it could be worse.' The vet finished his examination and reached for a syringe. 'I'm going to give him some antibiotics for that infection in his ear but apart from that all he needs is love and attention. And a bath.'

'Great.' Mac raked long fingers through his damp hair and wondered what was happening to his life. 'Is there a collar? Any clue as to an owner?'

'None. If you ask me, this dog's a stray,' the vet said firmly, dropping the syringe back on the tray. 'Probably bought as an early Christmas present and proved to be a handful. That's what usually happens. We'll send him to the local animal shelter and see if they can find him a home, but don't hold out too much hope. At this time of year there's a surplus of unwanted dogs.'

Louisa looked horrified. 'We're not taking him to the shelter,' she breathed, and Mac closed his eyes briefly, sensing what was coming.

'Louisa—'

'You can't let him go there,' she pleaded, her dark eyes huge as she looked at him. 'It's Christmas.'

'Louisa, it's a *dog*.'

'It's been abandoned.' There was a choke in her voice and a shine in her eyes that he struggled valiantly to ignore. 'He's *homeless*. Unloved.'

The vet grinned at Mac who gritted his teeth. 'There's no room in my life for a dog. I am not running a home for waifs and strays.'

'You live in a massive house. How much more room do you need? And if you're worried about the work, I'll look after him,' Louisa said immediately, and Mac ran a hand over the back of his neck. Never in his life had he found it so hard to say no to anyone, but there was something about those soft brown eyes that finished him off.

She was more pathetic than the dog.

'Louisa.' He hardened his tone. 'You're only here for a month.'

'I'll take him with me when I go. *Please*, Mac. He won't be any trouble.'

Mac looked at the dog, took in the size of its paws and the length of its shaggy body. 'He's going to be a bundle of trouble.'

Louisa gave a wobbly smile and stroked the dog's head. He thumped his tail weakly in response. 'He deserves a chance. And it is Christmas.'

Her voice cracked slightly and Mac felt his resolve weaken further. He'd never been remotely moved by feminine tears, but with Louisa it was different. Logic and common sense died a death. There was something about her that got to him and he didn't understand it. 'All right.' His tone was exasperated. 'We'll take him home. But this is just temporary, Louisa. As soon as he's recovered, we find him a proper home.'

'Oh, thank you, thank you.' She stood on tiptoe, flung her arms round his neck and hugged him tightly, and Mac felt something unravel inside him.

How long had it been since someone had hugged him like that?

He felt the brush of her soft hair against his cheek, the push of her full breasts against his chest, and breathed in her tantalising smell.

Damn.

He was about to step backwards when she removed her arms and turned towards the vet, her eyes shining. 'How much do we owe you?'

The vet named a figure that made Mac blink. *'How much?'*

He was just considering changing his profession when he realised that Louisa was tugging at his sleeve. 'You'll have to lend me the money,' she was saying to him, 'but I'll pay you back, I promise.'

He must be nuts.

'So not only do I have the bedraggled creature in my car, but I have to pay for the privilege,' he drawled as he reached for his wallet and dutifully produced his credit card. 'I thought you were supposed to be improving my life.'

'I am improving your life.' She stroked the dog's head with a gentle hand and the animal thumped its tail weakly. 'You're going to have a lovely warm feeling from doing the right thing. And while you're flexing your credit card, you might as well buy him an early Christmas present and get him a basket and some doggy stuff. I saw some things in Reception.'

Mac rolled his eyes and signed the bill, and together they carried the dog back to the car and tucked him up on the back seat, along with his new belongings.

'That dog is more comfortable than us,' Mac muttered, tucking the blanket around the injured animal and shaking his head in disbelief. 'I can't believe I'm doing this.'

'Neither can I, but I'm proud of you,' Louisa said happily, blowing on her fingers as she settled herself next to the dog. 'Look, he's thumping his tail. He knows he's safe now. Isn't that lovely?'

'Amazing,' Mac said dryly. 'What are you going to call him? Bedraggled?'

Louisa smiled, her hand on the dog's head. 'I'm going to call him Hopeful,' she said softly, 'because that's what he is.'

CHAPTER FIVE

HOPEFUL created havoc.

Bathed and fed by a doting Louisa, he soon regained his energy and took to bounding around the enormous garden and then into the house, leaving muddy pawprints over the floor.

'He makes more mess than us,' Josh said in disbelief as he watched Louisa scrubbing the hall floor three days later. 'That's the fourth time today you've done that. Hand me a cloth. I'll do the walls.'

'Better still, tie the cloth to his tail and he can do the walls himself,' Mac suggested dryly as he watched the chaos with weary amusement. 'I've never known a dog wag its tail so much.'

'It's because he's happy and he knows we saved him,' Louisa said happily, scrubbing hard at a stubborn muddy patch. 'He's showing us that he likes it here.'

Josh gave a snort. 'Well, of course he likes it here! Warm bed, regular meals. Dammit, *I* like it here. Or I did before the place was taken over by a hyperactive canine.'

Louisa dropped the cloth in the bucket and scrambled to her feet, her cheeks flushed and her eyes shining. 'Isn't he brilliant? He'll make an excellent guard dog while we're all at work.'

'Based on what?' Josh looked at her, his expression

comical. 'His ability to bash someone to death with his tail?'

'He has a ferocious bark,' Louisa said primly, 'and he knows his territory.'

And she adored him.

Mac rubbed long fingers over his forehead. 'My house used to be a peaceful sanctuary,' he muttered, 'and then you sent me Louisa as a Christmas present. Thanks, Josh. Great move.'

But there was humour in his eyes and something else that made Louisa's heart skip a beat. Since that moment in Resus she'd been careful to keep her distance. Careful not to crowd him in any personal sense. But the awareness between them was growing by the minute. When he entered the room her spine tingled and her pulse increased alarmingly.

'Dinner's in the Aga, guys,' she said huskily, burying her face in Hopeful's coat and giving him a hug. 'Help yourselves. I just need to shower and I'll be down.'

It was great to have both of them home. Often when they weren't at the hospital, they were on the beach windsurfing and the utility room was always full of dripping wetsuits. And she loved the lifestyle. She loved being able to wander into the rambling garden and down onto the sand. She loved being able to sit on the beach and watch the waves thrash against the rocks. She loved watching Mac and Josh powering across the bay at speeds that made her gasp.

She loved everything about the place.

Looking forward to a nice evening, she sprinted upstairs to her room, closely followed by Hopeful. 'You're not supposed to be upstairs,' she scolded gently, reaching down to stroke his head as he licked her hand. 'Go downstairs. Kitchen.'

Hopeful ignored her and sat down with a plop, his tongue lolling out of his mouth.

Louisa sighed and dragged her muddy sweatshirt over her head. 'OK, but just this once. And stay off the bed or Mac will kill you. And then he'll kill me.' She stepped into the bathroom, showered quickly and pulled on a clean pair of jeans and a jumper.

She was about to dry her hair when there was a tap on the door. 'Lu?' Josh's voice came through the doorway. 'Phone for you.'

Louisa sprinted downstairs to take the call, her dark hair hanging wetly down her back, Hopeful close on her heels. 'Hello?' She listened and then smiled. 'Alice? How are you? How's the wrist?' Her smile faded and she frowned. 'She what? Just now? Oh, no!'

Mac glanced up with a frown. 'What?'

Louisa covered the receiver. 'Vera has fallen downstairs. Alice can't move her. She's called an ambulance but they've said they can't get anyone to her for half an hour at least, and she's panicking.'

Mac didn't hesitate. 'We'll go round there now. Josh?'

'Right with you, bro.' Josh abandoned his casserole and stood up. 'We'll take my car.'

'The Maserati?' Mac gave a snort of derision. 'Don't be ridiculous. The roads are so slick we'll end up needing the ambulance ourselves. We need a four-wheel-drive. We'll take mine.'

'What's wrong with mine? She handles fine on the ice.' Josh looked offended. 'You're becoming middle-aged, do you know that?'

'Blame Louisa,' Mac said dryly, 'I used to be unencumbered but suddenly I seem to have all sorts of responsibilities. One of which is currently chewing your fancy shoes, Josh. Louisa, do something about your wet hair or you'll catch pneumonia.'

Josh turned in time to see Hopeful lumbering away with a shoe in his mouth.

'Stop arguing.' Louisa stuffed her hair into a wool hat, reached for her coat and made for the front door. 'Hopeful, on guard! You're in charge.'

Mac rolled his eyes. 'Heaven help us all.'

Vera was lying at the bottom of the stairs, her face white with pain.

Mac was beside her in an instant, his handsome face concerned. 'Hello, Vera, what have you been up to?'

Vera winced with pain. 'Oh, I'm so sorry to be a bother, only Alice thought it would be all right to call Louisa. I didn't know you came out to patients.'

Mac glanced at Louisa and gave a ghost of a smile. 'I don't usually but we're neighbours, so that's different,' he said softly, shrugging off his coat and bending down so that he could take a closer look. 'I don't want to move you until I've assessed the damage. Can you remember what happened?'

Vera closed her eyes. 'Stupid really. I was upstairs, pottering around, and decided that I wanted a glass of water.'

'You should have asked me,' Alice scolded. 'I would have fetched it for you.'

'You've broken your wrist,' Vera reminded her gruffly, opening her eyes and looking at her sister.

'You don't need to be waiting on me. I was trying to do it for myself.'

'You missed your footing?' Mac interrupted gently, and Vera nodded.

'One minute I was at the top, the next at the bottom.'

Mac frowned. 'Do you remember what happened? Were you knocked out?'

'She definitely wasn't,' Alice said firmly. 'She was using some language I didn't know she knew!'

Mac smiled and turned his attention back to his patient. 'Her left leg is shortened and externally rotated,' he said to Josh and his brother nodded.

'Looks like a fractured neck of femur.'

Alice gasped. 'She's broken something?'

'I think she might have done,' Mac said, examining the old lady gently but thoroughly. 'Does it hurt here?'

Vera groaned. 'Terribly. But maybe I'm just a wimp.'

'You're not a wimp,' Louisa soothed, her expression troubled. 'You're very brave. Just hang in there and Dr Sullivan will get you sorted out. He's a genius.'

Mac threw her a look, finished his examination and then straightened and dug in his pocket for his mobile phone. 'Let's see if we can hurry them along, Vera,' he said, his tone even as he hit the buttons. 'We need to get you to hospital. In the meantime, we're going to give you something for the pain and splint that leg.'

Vera sighed. 'It's definitely broken?'

Mac hesitated. 'I'm afraid so. But we'll soon have you more comfortable.'

'I don't want to go into hospital,' Vera said anxiously. 'I'm supposed to be cooking Christmas dinner now Alice is out of action. I've been reading books so that I know how to do it. I'm not the cook, you see. That's her job but with her wrist in a cast she can't do it.'

Louisa dropped to her knees. 'Don't worry about Christmas dinner,' she said firmly. 'Let's just sort your leg out and then we'll take care of the rest.'

'No, you don't understand.' Vera's tone was anguished. 'It isn't just the food. I can't leave Alice here on her own. She's never had Christmas on her own. It would be too awful. We always spend it together.'

'She won't be on her own,' Louisa said firmly, ignoring Mac's sharp glance. 'She can have Christmas lunch with us. I'm cooking a turkey and it's so large I don't know what I'm going to do with it. Josh will pick her up in his fancy car and bring her over.'

Mac closed his eyes and Josh choked with laughter.

'Just be warned, you'll be fighting off a brainless dog,' he drawled, 'so if you think this is going to be a peaceful Christmas, Alice, think again. You might want to think up some excuses.'

'Peaceful Christmas?' Mac's tone was dry as he looked at Louisa with an expression somewhere between exasperation and amusement. 'What's that?'

She grinned. 'It's what you used to have before I fell through your toilet window.'

'You fell through his toilet window?' Vera looked startled and Alice smiled.

'Remember, I told you that the doctor is living with someone now? It's so romantic.'

Mac muttered under his breath.

'It's a long story, Vera,' Louisa said happily, 'and I'll tell it over a glass of hot mulled wine on Christmas Day when I come to visit you in hospital. I do a fantastic turkey and stuffing sandwich.'

Still laughing, Josh handed Mac a syringe. 'I reckon she's the best Christmas present I've ever given you.'

'She's certainly the most memorable Christmas present you've ever given me. I'm just going to give you an injection for the pain, Vera,' Mac said calmly, moving her nightie aside, 'and then we're going to splint this leg to make it more comfortable. It will speed things up when the paramedics eventually get here.'

Louisa carried on chatting, distracting the two old ladies while the two brothers worked.

'All right.' Mac handed the empty syringe back to his brother. 'Now we're going to immobilise the leg, Vera. Josh, what have you got in your bag of tricks?'

'We could do a figure-of-eight bandage around the ankles and use triangular bandages for padding,' Josh muttered, delving in his bag and pulling out various bits and pieces.

'Great.' Mac reached for the triangular bandages and rolled them up. 'I'm going to use these as padding, Vera, and then I'm going to bandage your ankles to give you some support.'

Louisa stood up. 'While we're waiting for the ambulance, I'm just going to check upstairs that the lighting is good and that the carpet isn't worn. I want to check that you didn't fall over anything, Vera.'

She didn't want the same thing happening to Alice.

'Good thinking.' Mac shot her a look of approval and she blushed.

Bother.

He only had to glance in her direction and she turned into a jittery teenager in the throes of her first crush.

What was happening to her? Usually she found it all too easy to keep men at a distance. But with Mac it was different. *Everything felt different.*

Trying not to think about what her reaction might mean, she sprinted up the stairs and flicked on the light, squinting up at the bulb.

'Well, the light's strong enough and the carpet is fine,' she said eventually, 'but this rug is lifting at the corners. Could you have caught your foot on it, Vera?'

'I don't know,' Vera said weakly. 'Maybe. Silly me.'

'What were you wearing on your feet?' Mac's tone was even and Alice clucked.

'Those stupid slippers! I've told you to throw them away so many times.'

'And you were right as usual.' Vera closed her eyes and Mac frowned.

'How's the pain?'

'I'll cope.'

'In other words, it's bad,' he said softly. 'You'll be more comfortable as soon as we get you to hospital. I can give you something else.'

'I'm going to roll up this rug and put it out of the way,' Louisa called, stooping to remove the rug just as the ambulance arrived with the stretcher.

Alice was hovering anxiously. 'Can I go with her to the hospital?'

Josh nodded. 'I'll give you a lift. Mac?'

'I'll go in the ambulance.'

Louisa came back down the stairs and looked at him in surprise. For someone who claimed not to have time to worry about what happened to patients outside the department, he was showing an admirable degree of concern for Vera.

She cadged a lift in the ambulance with Mac, noticing how kind he was to the old lady. He helped the paramedics make her comfortable and then gently placed an oxygen mask over her face.

'Just breathe normally, Vera,' he instructed quietly, 'it will help.'

'You're a dear boy,' Vera murmured, patting his hand, 'and I'm so glad you're living with Louisa. It's time. After my Fred died I could never imagine finding anyone else and now, of course, I'm too old for anyone to look at me. I'm so pleased for you. You deserve to meet a nice girl.'

Mac opened his mouth and closed it again. 'Just try and relax,' he said gruffly, as he threw Louisa a baleful look.

She gave a weak smile. *He was going to kill her later.*

They arrived in A and E and Vera grabbed Mac's hand. 'Are you going to stay with me? I trust you.'

Louisa watched as something flickered across Mac's face. Then his hand wrapped around the old lady's. 'I'm staying,' he said gruffly, and Vera closed her eyes with a smile.

'That's all right, then.'

Observing the interaction between them, Louisa gave a soft smile of satisfaction. Unless she was mistaken, Mac Sullivan was allowing himself to develop an emotional connection. His icy remoteness was slipping.

He instructed the paramedics to take her into Resus and issued a set of instructions to the team who gathered. 'This is Vera. She has a suspected fractured femur.' He turned to the radiologist. 'I want an AP pelvis and lateral hip X-ray of the right side to start with. Let's get a line in and send some blood for U and Es, FBC, glucose and cross-match. She had analgesia at the scene but she's still in pain so I want to give her some more. Louisa...' He glanced up. 'Can you arrange an ECG? Just a precaution.'

Everyone set to work and Josh strolled in. 'How's it going? Alice is in the waiting room. Needless to say, she's worried.'

'Everything's in hand,' Mac murmured, checking the ECG carefully and giving a nod. 'That's fine. Has someone bleeped the orthopods?'

'I did it,' Louisa said, hurrying over to Josh. 'I'll go and talk to Alice. She must be worried sick.'

Mac stared at the X-rays through narrowed eyes, aware that Louisa's gaze was fixed expectantly on his face. *And he was struggling to concentrate.* He felt the brush of her arm against his and caught the worried expression on her face as she waited for his verdict.

'Well?' Her tone was urgent. 'What are you looking for?'

He dragged his eyes away from her soft mouth with

difficulty and concentrated on the films in front of him.

'Disruption of the trabeculae, inferior or superior cortices and abnormality of the pelvic contours.' He lifted a finger and trailed it down the line of the bone to illustrate his point. 'If you look here, you can see that the trabeculae are angulated but the inferior cortex is intact. There's no significant displacement. It's classified as a Garden 1 fracture.'

Why was he noticing her?

He made a point of never noticing women.

Especially not women like Louisa. She was lonely and the only relationship she wanted involved diamonds. And he was no good at that sort of relationship.

He turned as the orthopaedic registrar walked up behind him. 'Ken.' He gave a brief nod, grateful for the interruption. 'Got a patient for you.'

The orthopaedic reg stared at the X-rays. 'So you have.'

Louisa bit her lip. 'Will she be in hospital over Christmas?'

All she thought about was the personal, Mac mused, casting a curious glance in her direction. To her a patient wasn't just an injury to be put right but a whole person with problems. He'd never met anyone quite like her.

'Afraid so.' Ken tugged the X-rays out of the light box and gave a rueful smile. 'But don't worry about it. The orthopaedic ward is the next best thing to Christmas in Lapland.'

'You mean you're economising on heating?' Louisa lifted an eyebrow and he grinned.

'No, I don't mean that. But our ward sister got a little carried away with the decorations this year and the place looks like Santa's grotto.'

Louisa gave a delighted smile. 'That's excellent.'

Mac rolled his eyes and handed over the notes. 'Don't give her ideas. At the moment my department still looks suitably clinical and I'd like it to stay that way. Vera's all yours, Ken. Look after her.'

They dropped Alice home, checked that she had food and that she was all right and then drove back to the house.

Glancing at Mac's tense profile, Louisa bit her lip. 'Are you angry with me?'

'Why? For inviting her to spend Christmas with us? Or because the entire village now thinks you're living with me? You've invaded my privacy, taken over my house, introduced a mad dog to my life and given out my home number to patients. Why would I be angry with you?'

She face fell. *She'd ruined his evening.* 'I didn't mean to interfere.'

'Yes, you did. It's what you do best.' There was a gleam in his dark eyes. 'And you did the right thing, giving the number to Alice. I'm glad she called. I wouldn't have wanted Vera to be lying there waiting for the paramedics to show up. At least we were able to make her more comfortable.'

Her face brightened. 'You're not angry?'

'For dragging me away from my dinner to administer first aid?' He shook his head and changed gear. 'No. But I'm not so sure about the dog. You might still live to regret that bit.'

Was he teasing her? 'We couldn't just leave him, Mac.'

'Correction,' he drawled softly, '*you* couldn't just leave him. But you couldn't leave anything, could you, Louisa? Not if it was in trouble. Josh said you were a fixer and now I see what he means.'

She frowned. 'If you're trying to convince me that you would have dumped that dog in some rotten home, I don't believe you. You put on this tough, macho, independent act, but underneath you're a big softie.'

'Louisa—'

'I saw you with Vera,' she said breathlessly. 'You *cared* about her.'

'I never said I didn't care about the patients,' he said evenly, 'just that I wasn't prepared to take on all of their problems outside the hospital. And I stand by that. We can only do so much, Louisa.'

'I know, and I do find that hard. I hated leaving Alice in the house on her own tonight,' Louisa muttered, and Mac sighed.

'At least you didn't ask her to move in with us. Thank you for that.'

Louisa peeped at him guiltily. 'I *almost* did.'

'I know.' His hands tightened on the wheel. 'And I'm relieved you managed to contain yourself for once or Hopeful might have been jealous. Vera will be all right. People are tougher than they look.'

Louisa glanced at him, taking in his strong profile, the hard lines of his cheeks and jaw. *He was all man.* 'They've never been separated, you know. They do everything together.'

Mac gritted his teeth. 'You cannot take on everyone's problems! You can't rescue everyone, Louisa. You're interfering again.'

'Interfering is the one thing I do really well,' she said simply. 'It's my talent.'

'People sing or play the piano,' Mac said dryly. 'That's talent. Meddling in people's lives is something else, although in this instance I admit your interfering nature paid off. If you hadn't made a friend of Alice and given her the number, she wouldn't have called the house and then goodness knows what state poor Vera would have been in by the time the ambulance arrived.'

'You see?' Louisa's tone was triumphant. 'You pretend you don't care about your patients as people, but you do.'

She knew he cared. She'd seen it in his eyes and in the way he'd been so gentle with Vera.

'I care, Louisa. Just don't invite Alice to live with us,' Mac warned, drawing up outside the house and switching off the engine. 'That dog is enough.'

They walked into the house to discover that 'that dog' had emptied the remains of the casserole onto the kitchen floor and eaten it.

'Oh, my goodness…' Louisa gasped as she surveyed the upturned casserole on the kitchen floor. 'He must have knocked it off the table.'

'Now we know why he was abandoned,' Mac muttered, and Louisa threw him a reproachful look.

'He'll be fine when he's trained.'

Hopeful chose that particular moment to charge into the kitchen, stumbling over his giant paws as he rushed to greet Louisa. He launched himself into space, tail wagging, and knocked her flat on her back.

'Ow.'

'Louisa.' Mac's tone was patient as he jabbed long fingers through his dark hair and watched with something between amusement and exasperation. 'That dog has a brain the size of a pea. You will never be able to train him. Personally I would have named him Clueless.'

Laughing helplessly, Louisa gave Hopeful a push and struggled upright, her dark hair tumbling over her eyes. She brushed it away and reached out to retrieve the empty casserole dish from the floor. 'At least he enjoyed it. He's eaten the lot.' She couldn't stop laughing and Mac rolled his eyes.

'I'm so pleased.'

She struggled to her feet, dumped the dish in the sink and turned on the taps. 'Isn't he funny?'

'Hilarious.' Mac dropped onto the nearest chair and closed his eyes. 'I'm knackered. My life used to be calm and ordered. Then you arrived.'

Louisa glanced towards him, her expression suddenly contrite. 'You poor thing. I'd forgot what a long day you've had. I'll make you some hot chocolate and tuck you into bed.'

'Tuck me into bed?' His eyes opened and clashed with hers and she felt her colour build.

His gaze was intent, *male...*

'I didn't exactly mean...' Thoroughly unsettled, she turned around sharply and knocked a saucepan off the side. 'Oops—clumsy me.'

'You're as bad as Hopeful,' he murmured, standing up and walking towards her. 'Hot chocolate sounds good, although I don't know why. It's nursery food and not something I usually drink.' He was so close that she couldn't breathe properly. 'But, then, you're making me do a lot of things I don't usually do. Why's that, I wonder?'

The soft wool of his black jumper clung gently to the hard muscle of his shoulders and she stared in fascination at the dark shadow on his jaw.

'It's just my naturally interfering nature,' she muttered, her legs suddenly threatening to give way. *This close she was aware of every tantalising inch of him.*

He stared at her for a moment and then gave her a slow, sexy smile. 'I'll take you up on the offer of hot chocolate but I'll tuck myself in,' he drawled softly. 'I think it would be safer for both of us that way.'

She swallowed, trapped by the look in his eyes. 'Absolutely.'

She was desperate for him to kiss her.

'Louisa.' His voice was rough. 'Stop looking at me like that. You did it the other day in Resus.'

She swallowed hard. 'Sorry.'

His eyes drifted to her mouth. 'I'm not your type, remember?'

Her heart was pounding against her chest. 'What would you say if I told you I might have been wrong about that?'

There was a long, aching silence and then finally his eyes lifted to hers. 'I'd say that we'd both be in trouble.'

'Why?'

He gave a crooked smile and brushed her cheek with his fingers. 'Because you want happy ever after and that's the one thing I don't do. Go to bed, Louisa. And lock your door.'

CHAPTER SIX

LOUISA woke late.

She padded over to the window and discovered that more snow had fallen in the night. The garden was white, the wind was whipping the sea into a frenzy and the sky was grey and threatening.

And she could see a lone windsurfer out on the waves.

Mac?

Remembering the tension that had flared between them the night before, she gave a little shiver. Then she reached for her clothes and pulled them on quickly. She was on a late shift so she still had time for a walk.

Scooping her hair under a hat, she whistled for Hopeful, pulled on a coat and boots and made for the beach.

It had nothing to do with the fact that Mac was windsurfing, she told herself firmly as she put Hopeful's lead in her pocket. It was just that she needed some fresh air before she started her shift.

She opened the back door and gasped as the cold air hit her. Hopeful barked happily and bounded down the garden and onto the beach.

Louisa followed more slowly, cuddling her coat around her, feeling the cold biting into her cheeks as she watched the windsurfer scoot across the waves, driven by the winter wind.

It felt good to be outside. She wandered along the shore, Hopeful dancing around her feet, her eyes on the sea.

As she reached the water's edge, Mac was dragging his board onto the sand. 'I don't know how you can do that in this weather.' She stared at the sea and shivered.

His eyes gleamed and droplets of water clung to his dark jaw. 'This is the best kind of weather.'

'You could get blown over to France.'

He lifted the board with a smile. 'Onshore wind, Louisa.' His muscles flexed hard under the wetsuit. 'I'd be blown back onto the beach.'

She laughed and walked with him along the sand. 'I don't know much about the sea. Have you lived here all your life?'

'My parents had a house further down the coast. Dad sailed. My uncle built boats. Josh and I were brought up on the water.'

It sounded good.

'You're lucky to have a brother. I always wanted a sibling. Someone to share things with.'

They were back at the house now and she watched while Mac stowed the windsurfer. 'We weren't that great at sharing.' He unzipped the neck of his wetsuit and she felt her breath catch. 'Whatever I had, Josh wanted. Just typical brothers, I suppose.'

It sounded good to her. Sibling rivalry. The security of family.

'He loves you.' She dragged the hat off her head and her dark hair tumbled down her back. 'He's worried about you. That's why he asked me to come.'

His gaze lingered on her hair and then his eyes

clashed with hers. 'I don't think you're the answer to my problems, Louisa.' His voice was deep and very male. 'And I know for sure I'm not the answer to yours.'

'Louisa? Louisa, *are you listening to me*?'

Louisa blinked and looked at Hannah. 'Sorry? Did you say something?'

'Only about five times.' Hannah rolled her eyes and slammed her locker shut. 'You were on another planet.'

Louisa felt hot colour seep into her cheeks. 'I was thinking about something.'

'Something or someone?' Hannah gave a sympathetic smile. 'He's gorgeous, I'll give you that, but don't hold your breath. I'd hate to see you hurt, and Mac Sullivan is married to his job.'

But why? Apart from work and windsurfing, which appeared to be a solitary sport, he did nothing. It was almost as if he didn't allow himself a social life, Louisa mused as she locked her bag away and followed Hannah out of the staffroom. And he refused to talk about his wife. Or even look at another woman.

She sighed. He must have loved her very much.

He obviously thought he couldn't enjoy himself any more. It was up to her to show him differently.

'Hannah...' She looked at her friend thoughtfully. 'You know the Christmas party...'

'The hospital one?' Hannah pocketed her scissors. 'It's great. They hold it in the post-grad centre two days before Christmas. Lots of free food and drink, the chief executive wearing antlers and everyone getting drunk and regretting it madly the day afterwards. You know the sort of thing.'

Louisa grinned. 'I certainly do.' Her smile faded. 'I was thinking I might invite Mac.'

Hannah's eyes widened. 'He never goes. He's always working.'

'Well, this year Josh is the one working,' Louisa said breathlessly, 'because I already checked. So theoretically he could go.'

Hannah stared at her. 'How are you going to persuade him?'

'I don't know yet,' Louisa confessed, 'but I'm working on it.'

Hannah shrugged. 'Well, it's a good excuse to dress up and sparkle. Maybe you could seduce him.'

Louisa thought of her wardrobe and pulled a face. 'That might be a problem. Everything in my wardrobe is thermal at the moment.'

And she'd never seduced anyone in her life before.

'There's a great dress shop right on the quay,' Hannah said helpfully as they walked through the department. 'You should be able to find something to wow him.'

A slow smile spread across Louisa's face. 'I might just do that.'

'At least you've got someone to lust after,' Hannah said gloomily. 'I've given up finding anyone that makes my pulse race. The way I'm going, I'll be stuck working on my own in A and E until I'm ninety.'

At that moment the doors to the ambulance bay crashed open behind them and a young man ran in, carrying a child in his arms. 'Help me! She's choking!' He looked round, worry etched on his features, and then he spotted Louisa. 'She can't breathe—do something!

Louisa took one look at the child. 'Quick—bring her into Resus. Hannah—call Mac.' She took the child from the father and quickly knelt on the floor, laying the child over her knees with her head lower than her back. 'What's her name?'

'Poppy.' The father jammed his fingers through his hair, his eyes wild with panic as he looked at his child. 'Is she going to die?'

'Try and calm down,' Louisa urged gently, delivering five sharp blows to the child's back while her thighs supported the child. 'Poppy? Poppy, I want you to cough—that's it. Good girl. Do you have any idea what she swallowed?'

'No.' The father shook his head, sucking in air in an effort to gain control. 'One minute she was playing with her toys on the carpet and the next she made a weird sound and started choking.'

The doors to Resus swung open and Mac strode in with Hannah. 'What's happening?'

'Choking on a foreign body,' Louisa said quickly, 'she's still breathing and she's coughing but so far she hasn't managed to clear it. I've tried back blows.'

'Try chest thrusts,' Mac said immediately, stepping forward and taking over. 'Do we know what she's swallowed?'

'It could be anything,' the father said as he paced backwards and forwards across the room, frantic with worry. 'She had a whole pile of toys. She was really happy…' His voice cracked and Mac shot Hannah a meaningful glance.

She stepped up to the father and touched his arm gently. 'This is very distressing for you. Why don't you wait outside?'

'No!' He shook off her arm in a violent movement. 'I'm not leaving her. I want to stay. She needs me.' His face contorted with guilt and panic. 'This is all my fault.'

'Children swallow things,' Louisa said soothingly, helping Mac shift the child's position so that he could administer chest thrusts. 'It happens. You mustn't blame yourself.'

He was so obviously traumatised by the whole episode that she felt her heart twist with sympathy. Where was the child's mother? she wondered.

'I should have been watching…'

Despite Mac's efforts, the child continued to choke and Mac lifted her into his arms and laid her gently on the trolley.

'Bleep the anaesthetist,' he instructed calmly, and Hannah left the room swiftly. 'Louisa, I want to check her mouth. Get me a laryngoscope and a pair of McGill's forceps.'

Louisa lifted the choking child, noticing that her colour was worse. She lifted her gaze to Mac and he gave a brief nod of understanding.

'I'm going to try abdominal thrusts. Let's have her supine.' He placed the heel of one hand on the upper abdomen and gave five sharp thrusts up towards the diaphragm but the little girl continued to choke.

Hannah hurried back into the room. 'Anaesthetist on his way.'

'Can't wait,' Mac muttered, his eyes still on the child. 'Laryngoscope.'

Louisa placed it in his hand and held her breath while Mac tilted the child's head back and tried to visualise the obstruction. 'There's nothing— Oh, wait a minute…' He squinted and then held out his other hand. 'I see something… Give me those forceps, Louisa.'

She did as he asked and watched while he carefully inserted them into the child's throat. 'That's it!' He withdrew the forceps, dropped the foreign body into the dish that Louisa was holding out for him and then exhaled slowly. 'Let's give her some oxygen.'

Thank goodness.

Louisa felt her knees weaken with relief.

It had been a close thing. A few minutes more and they would have had to perform a tracheostomy.

The father stepped forward, his face chalk white as he stared into the dish. 'A toy?' He sagged slightly. 'She swallowed a toy. Oh, no…'

Louisa registered his pallor, saw him sway and frowned in consternation. 'Are you all right?'

'Come and sit down,' Hannah said quickly, interpreting Louisa's glance. 'You've had a fright. We don't want you fainting.' She pushed him into a chair and kept her hand on his shoulder. 'It's Rick, isn't it? Rick Matthews? I recognise you now. You own the garage on the high street.'

The man inhaled deeply, his elbows on his thighs, his face still pale and drawn. 'That's right.' He looked up at Hannah, no recognition in his eyes.

'I'm Hannah.' She crouched down beside him, her hand still on his shoulder. 'You fixed my car for me last winter. Saved my life.'

He looked at her blankly. 'Did I?'

'You certainly did.' Hannah gave him a warm smile. 'Calm down, Rick. Poppy is going to be fine.'

Rick closed his eyes and shook his head slowly. 'I'm a terrible father.'

'You're a great father.' Hannah took his hand in hers. 'When I brought my car in I remember you telling me that you had a little girl. That you were on your own with her. That must be very hard for you.'

This was one of the advantages of living and working in a small community, Louisa thought as she listened. Hannah knew about this man. He'd helped her and now she was helping him. The knowledge gave her a warm feeling. Wasn't that what Christmas was all about?

'My wife left a year ago.' His expression was bleak. 'I thought we were doing OK. I thought I could do everything a woman could do…' His expression was anguished and Mac looked up and frowned.

'Children have accidents, Rick. It's a fact of life. We can try and prevent them but they still happen.'

Rick shook his head. 'I failed her…'

'You brought her here straight away,' Hannah said calmly, her hand still on his arm. 'You didn't fail her. You did the right thing.'

Rick stared at his daughter, now breathing easily on the trolley under Mac's eagle eye. 'I always think a mother could do it better. Especially at this time of year. I tried to cook turkey last year and it was a disaster. I didn't cook it for long enough and the oven was too high. It was burned on the outside and raw in the middle. We ended up eating baked beans.' He gave a helpless shrug and looked at them. 'How do people do it? I mean, are you born knowing how to cook a turkey?'

'Certainly not,' Mac said dryly. 'I wouldn't have a clue how to cook a turkey.'

Louisa bit her lip. 'I'm great at cooking turkey. I'll do you a deal,' she said impulsively, turning towards Rick, 'I'll cook your Christmas lunch if you'll fix my car.' She heard Mac inhale sharply. 'You can come to us for Christmas Day.'

As far as she was concerned, the more the merrier.

Rick gave a disbelieving laugh. 'You're offering to have us for Christmas? Why would you do that?'

'Because she just can't help it,' Mac muttered under his breath, and Louisa ignored him.

'Because I've ordered a turkey that would feed the whole of Cornwall and because I need my car fixed. You have no idea how to cook a turkey but I have absolutely no idea why my car hates cold weather. I'm hopeless. I can't even open the bonnet.' She shrugged helplessly. 'So—is it a deal?'

Rick looked towards Hannah and Louisa was struck with inspiration. 'Hannah's coming, too,' she said firmly, 'as soon as she finishes her early shift.'

Hannah gave a delighted nod of acknowledgement and Mac closed his eyes for a brief moment.

At that moment Poppy struggled to sit up and Mac removed the oxygen mask from her face so that she could speak.

'Can we, Daddy?' Her voice was hoarse and weak and Rick breathed out slowly, his eyes shining with love as he looked at his daughter.

'Well…' His face broke into a smile. 'Well, yes, it is. Why not? Thanks. Thanks a lot.'

Louisa grinned. 'Don't thank me yet. You haven't seen the state of my car.'

'Whatever's wrong with it, I'll get it sorted for you,' Rick vowed, and Louisa nodded.

'I know you will.' She turned to the little girl. 'And now, Poppy, you'd better tell me what's on your Christmas list.'

At that moment the anaesthetist hurried into Resus. 'Did you bleep me?'

'Yes.' Mac straightened and ripped off his gloves. 'But we're fine here now, thankfully.' He glanced at Rick. 'Let her play with the toys here for half an hour—see how she goes, but there shouldn't be any ill effects. Hannah will stay with you. Louisa, I need a word with you outside.'

Louisa took one look at his grim profile and thought about refusing. Then she decided that she might as well face the music and followed him into the corridor.

'I know, I know,' she muttered. 'You're angry with me again.'

'Louisa, you can't just keep inviting total strangers for Christmas.' He paced up and down the corridor, his tone exasperated. 'I am not running some sort of hotel!'

'Alice isn't a stranger,' she protested, 'and neither is Hannah. And come to that, neither is Rick. He's local. His wife left him, Mac. He's struggling to have a family Christmas with his little girl. You can't cook a turkey for two people. It just doesn't work.'

Mac moved to one side as a nurse hurried past. 'Neither does inviting everyone to eat ours!' Aware that they were attracting attention, he lowered his voice. 'That doesn't work either. I'm not Santa! I don't even know them.'

'They live in the village,' she pointed out. 'If you had more time, I'm sure you'd know them. And you just saved his daughter's life. By the way, you were amazing.' Warmth flooded through her as she remembered just how calm he'd been. 'I could feel myself starting to panic but you were so focused.'

A muscle worked in his lean jaw. 'It's my job, Louisa. And stop trying to change the subject.'

'I'm not changing the subject. Well, maybe just a little.' She gave an impish grin. 'There are two things I probably ought to tell you so that you can get all your yelling over with in one go. The first is that Josh is giving me a lift home tonight. We're taking a bit of a detour.'

His eyes narrowed suspiciously and he stopped pacing. 'What sort of detour?'

Louisa braced herself. 'I want to buy a Christmas tree,' she said quickly. 'I noticed that they have beautiful ones along the coast road where we found Hopeful.'

He was going to say no.

He sighed and jabbed his fingers through his hair. 'You've already decorated my hallway. I don't need a tree.'

'But *I* do. It's part of my Christmas fantasy, you see. Big tree, holly and mistletoe. And Poppy will expect a tree. Every little girl wants a Christmas tree.'

He rolled his eyes. 'Who are you doing this for?' His tone was exasperated and he started pacing again. 'I don't need a tree. It will drop needles and make a mess.'

'Just a small one,' she wheedled, 'and there won't be any needles. Trees don't drop any more. Please? You won't regret it.'

He shot her a look that spoke volumes. 'That's what you said when you landed me with a dog.'

She grinned. 'Hopeful is going to love having a tree and Poppy is going to love Hopeful. That little girl is going to have a lovely Christmas.'

'Louisa!' Mac grabbed her by the shoulders and gave her a little shake. 'You can't bring together a bunch of individuals who don't know each other just because they happen to be lonely or hungry! We're all virtual strangers with separate lives. We probably have nothing in common! You can't just create the perfect Christmas by taking in waifs and strays! That isn't how it works!'

She felt the strength of his fingers digging through the thin fabric of her uniform. 'Why not?'

'Because Christmas is about family—'

'Not necessarily.' She shook her head. 'It's about sharing. And friendship. And about no one being alone. I didn't want Rick struggling on his own with little Poppy. I don't want Poppy missing her mother. And I didn't want Alice to be on her own in that big dark house surrounded by nothing but silence and memories. She needs noise and laughter and a big tree covered in lights. She needs people opening presents that they don't want and getting irritated with each other for talking too loudly at all the wrong times.'

Mac closed his eyes. 'This isn't happening to me.'

'It'll be fine. I'll choose a few presents to put under the tree,' Louisa said soothingly, 'so you're not to worry about a thing. Just turn up and eat my turkey.

All I expect you to do is carve. I can't carve to save my life. I never could have been a surgeon.'

'Louisa—'

She backed away quickly. 'Thanks, Mac. Got to dash. Josh is waiting.'

And she didn't want to give Mac the chance to say no.

Mac stared at the enormous tree in his living room and wondered what had happened to his life. Hopeful was running in circles around the sitting room, barking with excitement, every wag of his tail sending more pine needles cascading onto the floor.

'Louisa…' His voice was faint. 'You said a *small* tree.'

'Isn't it fantastic?' Louisa stood back, her eyes shining as she stared at the bushy branches. 'It's a fir. Josh spotted it. It's a wonderful shape.'

'It's massive. And it's dropping.' His eyes slid to the floor. 'You said it wouldn't drop. There are more needles on my floor than the tree.'

'That's just because of Hopeful and his tail. It's a beautiful tree,' Louisa said happily, and he stared at her, his attention caught by the shine in her eyes. She was like a child, excitement bubbling out of her like a fountain. Her cheeks were pink from the cold and she was still wearing a soft scarf looped round her neck as she secured the tree in the pot.

She was wearing a soft wool skirt and knee-length boots and her hair tumbled down her back in glorious waves.

Lust, powerful and primitive, thudded through his body and he gritted his teeth, resisting the temptation to push her against the nearest wall and kiss her breathless.

It would be a mistake.

Her dream was happy families, he reminded himself grimly as Hopeful did another circuit of the room, totally out of control. And he didn't do happy families.

And she didn't do lust under the Christmas tree.

Unfortunately for him, their Christmas wish lists didn't coincide. A relationship wasn't on his.

'Sit! You stupid dog.' Hopeful jumped up and licked him frantically and Mac pushed him away. 'Louisa, this dog needs a psychiatrist.'

'He's just excited about the tree,' she said soothingly, brushing her dark hair out of her eyes with a gloved hand. 'He'll calm down in a minute.'

'We've had him for seven days,' Mac was forced to point out, reaching out and grabbing Hopeful in an iron grip, 'and he hasn't calmed down yet.'

'He'll be fine when he's trained.'

Mac gave up. 'Where do you want these lights?' He released the dog with a warning glare that earned him a wagged tail. 'Anywhere in particular?'

'Oh…' She squinted at the tree through narrowed eyes and waved a hand vaguely. 'Wherever you think. And then we need to fetch your decorations.'

He twisted the lights around the tree. 'I don't have any decorations.'

'What, none?' He heard the shock in her voice and gave a wry smile.

'Louisa, this is the first year I've ever had a tree in this house.'

She stared at him. 'And how long have you lived here?'

He shrugged, suddenly feeling mildly uncomfortable. 'Six years.'

'Six years!' She sounded appalled. 'And you've never had a tree before?'

'I'm never here at Christmas.' He kept his tone patient. 'I'm always working.'

'Well, not for *all* of it,' she said, unlooping the scarf and dropping it on the floor beside her. 'No one can be working for *all* of it.'

Mac thought of the number of times he'd worked straight through the entire festive season, sleeping at the hospital so that others could have time off. 'Yes, they can.'

Her brown eyes held his. 'Only if they have a really, really good reason not to be at home.'

He tensed under her soft, searching gaze. 'Louisa…'

'What was your reason, Mac?'

He inhaled sharply and walked over to the window, keeping his back to her. 'My wife was usually working at Christmas, too.'

'I see.'

Her tone made it clear that she didn't see at all.

'We were busy,' he said gruffly, and she looked at him blankly.

'Busy.' She cleared her throat. 'Right.'

'Not everyone does Christmas, Louisa,' he said, his tone irritable. 'It's just another day of the year.'

'Well, this year you're going to be here,' she said firmly. 'You've got the day off. Josh is working and I need you to carve the turkey. I'm hopeless at carving, remember? I've checked the rota and I've worked it all out. We're going to have turkey and presents round the tree and Josh can join us later.'

Mac tried to think of the last time he'd eaten proper turkey at Christmas and gave up. 'I'm not that wild about turkey—'

'That's because you've never tasted mine.' She grinned at him and smacked her lips. 'It's not to be missed.'

'In that case, I'd better not miss it.'

It was just lunch, he told himself. And he didn't need to be sociable. He could just eat lunch and then disappear to the beach with his surfboard. If Louisa wanted a crowded, noisy Christmas full of people then she could have one. It didn't mean he had to be part of it.

'There's something else I wanted to ask you…' She kept her tone casual and he felt himself tense in readiness.

'Now what?' His tone was dry. 'You've invited the whole of the English rugby team along with everyone they've ever met in their lives?'

'Am I that bad?' She laughed and shook her head. 'No, I haven't invited anyone else. But I want to invite *you*—to the hospital Christmas party the day after tomorrow. Will you go?' She blushed prettily and brushed a strand of dark hair out of her eyes, 'Well what I mean really is, will you go with me? You're going to say no, I know you are.'

He opened his mouth to say exactly that. 'Yes, all right. Why not?'

There were a thousand reasons why he shouldn't,

but looking into her shining dark eyes he suddenly couldn't remember any of them.

'You'll go? Truly? Fab!' She jumped up, sending more pine needles flying, clearly as astonished as he was by his decision. 'I'm *so* pleased.'

Mac shook his head.

He must be losing all good sense. 'It will be cold sausage rolls and limp mince pies,' he warned gruffly. 'You could cook better yourself.'

Damn. He shouldn't have said yes. He didn't want her getting the wrong idea.

She clasped her hands together. 'I don't care about the food, Mac, I just want to dance.' A huge smile spread across her face. 'And you're going to dance with me.'

Something stirred inside him and he squashed it down ruthlessly.

'It isn't a date, Louisa.'

'Of course it's a date.' She winked at him. 'You'd better get some serious rest, Dr Sullivan,' she drawled, her eyes twinkling, 'otherwise I'm likely to exhaust you.'

Mac bit his lip and refrained from pointing out that there were other ways that she could exhaust him that he'd find far more satisfying.

And then his eyes drifted to the tree and he remembered that all she wanted was a family.

And that was the one thing he wasn't going to be able to give her.

Feeling daring, Louisa applied a touch of glitter to her hair and cheeks, put the finishing touches to her make-up and tried to control the churning of her stomach. There was nothing to be excited about. It wasn't even a proper date, she reasoned. All right, so they were going to the party together, but they weren't really *together*.

But at least he'd agreed to go with her so that was a start.

And his house was decorated and she'd ordered the turkey.

Louisa smiled at her reflection in the mirror. This year, like it or not, Mac Sullivan was going to do Christmas. And she was going to make sure that he enjoyed himself. Maybe then he'd stop shutting everyone out.

Maybe he'd even talk about his wife.

Or had he loved her so much he just couldn't face talking about her to anyone?

She stepped back and gazed at her reflection in the mirror. She'd followed Hannah's advice and paid a visit to the little shop on the quay, and she'd found the perfect dress. Or, at least, she hoped it was perfect.

Reaching for her coat and her bag, she left the bedroom and walked downstairs.

Mac was waiting for her in the hallway, flicking through the post.

He looked spectacular in a dinner jacket, she thought dreamily as she paused halfway down the stairs and said his name.

He glanced up and froze, his eyes fixed on her face for a long moment before travelling downwards, scrutinising every inch of her. He didn't speak and she suddenly felt self-conscious.

What if he hated the dress?

It *was* a bit daring at the front but she'd loved the colour so much…

'You look stunning. And you glitter like something off the Christmas tree.' His voice was husky and he dropped the post on the side and stepped forward.

'Are you ready?'

She smiled a womanly smile as she walked down the rest of the stairs and took his arm. 'Completely ready.'

CHAPTER SEVEN

THEY danced without stopping.

Once or twice Louisa noticed other women casting covetous glances towards Mac but he seemed totally unaware of the attention he was attracting from all the females in the room. Instead, he swung her this way and that as they moved in time to the music, his dark gaze fastened on her with a flattering degree of attentiveness.

He'd discarded his jacket and opened the top buttons of his shirt, exposing a hint of dark chest hair, and he moved with an easy rhythm, lithe and athletic and sexier than any man had a right to be. He looked dark, masculine and more than a little dangerous. Nothing like the remote, dedicated doctor she was used to working with.

Noticing another woman gazing longingly over her partner's shoulder towards Mac, Louisa resisted the temptation to drag him off the dance floor, take him home and lock him away.

He was staggeringly good-looking, she consoled herself, trying to ignore everyone around them. It was perfectly normal that women would stare. *She was struggling not to stare herself.* Mac was a man who would always stand out in a crowd. Everything about him was intensely masculine. The hard lines of his face, the darkness of his jaw and the power in his broad shoulders. He was a man who would always draw women. But for tonight, at least, he was with her.

They danced and danced until her feet ached and finally the music slowed and Mac slid an arm around her waist. He pulled her against him, his hold unmistakably possessive. 'Do you know that every man in the room is looking at you?'

Were they?

And Louisa realised that although she'd noticed the women, she hadn't noticed the men. For her there *were* no other men in the room. For her there was only Mac. *And Mac would always make other men fade into the background.*

She looked up at him, caught the lazy gleam in his dark eyes and felt her stomach turn over. 'My dress is probably too low…'

He smiled and his gaze dropped to her mouth. 'Your dress,' he drawled huskily, 'is perfect.'

The unexpected compliment made her pulse race and suddenly she found it hard to breathe properly. He was looking at her as if—*as if…*

A thrill of excitement rippled through her and for the first time in her life she discovered what it felt like to really, *really* want a man.

And be wanted in return.

Because he did want her. Of that she was sure.

His body felt hard and strong against hers and suddenly she never, ever wanted him to let her go. 'Are you hungry?'

They hadn't been near the buffet. From the moment they'd arrived they'd been on the dance floor, their attention focused only on each other.

'No.' His eyes glittered hard in the dim light. 'Are you?'

She felt the pressure of his hand on the small of her back, easing her closer still, and she closed her eyes and leaned her head against his chest. Her heart was pounding so wildly she assumed he must be able to feel it.

Suddenly the world around them faded away and all she was aware of was Mac.

The blood throbbed in her veins as she slid her arms around his neck. She felt his sudden stillness and then he tightened his hold.

She felt the press of his thighs against her, the solid muscle of his shoulders and the firm beat of his heart.

They moved together, instinctively matching each other's rhythm. Would it be like that in bed? she wondered, her whole body in a heightened state of sexual tension. She gave herself a little shake. *They weren't in bed,* she reminded herself firmly. They were on the dance floor in a very public place and she shouldn't be having those sorts of thoughts.

But how could she not?

Being held by Mac felt so *right*.

Locked in his arms, feeling his strength and breathing in that tantalising, elusive male scent, she felt safe, *and yet not safe*.

Mac Sullivan was holding back.

She thought about the layers. About the man. Underneath the rigid self-discipline lay scorching passion. He wouldn't be half-hearted, she knew that. He was a man who knew exactly what he wanted and wouldn't be afraid to go for it.

She looked up at him and stopped moving, suddenly trapped by the look in his eyes. Awareness flared between them, a mutual recognition of the sexual tension that had been building since they'd met.

Unable to help herself, Louisa lifted a hand to his cheek, feeling the warmth of his skin and the roughness of his jaw.

She wanted to touch him. *All of him.*

Something shifted his eyes and then, with a determined movement, Mac gently disengaged himself, closed his hand around her wrist and walked her purposefully towards the door.

There was no mistaking his intention and, like someone who has teased a tiger only to find that the cage door wasn't shut, Louisa felt her heart suddenly race in a mixture of pure excitement and panic.

She'd never done this before.

'Where are we going?' She paused, breathless, as he retrieved their coats, aware that people were watching them. Speculating.

'Home.'

'People are staring.'

He draped her coat over her shoulders, his eyes glittering as he looked at her. 'Let them stare.' He shrugged, totally cool and indifferent to everyone else in the room. 'I don't care much about what people think, you should know that by now.'

Without glancing left or right, he led her away from the party, down a brightly lit corridor and into the freezing night air.

Her heart was thumping so fast she could hardly breathe.

'People will gossip.'

There was a gleam of laughter in his eyes as he

glanced towards her. 'You should have thought of that before you posted yourself head first through my toilet window.' They had reached the car by now and he grabbed her and turned her quickly, his body trapping hers, his arms either side of her head, preventing her escape.

Not that she had any intention of escaping.

She was where she wanted to be.

His mouth was only inches from hers and she could see the thickness of his dark lashes, the strong, straight lines of his nose and the blue-black shadow of his jaw.

'If you don't want this, Louisa say so now.' His voice was forceful, husky, and she felt something curl low in her pelvis.

There was only one answer she could possibly give. 'I want this.'

His gaze burned into hers and his body pressed closer. 'You know I'm not making you promises. You know the sort of man I am.'

She knew.

Strong. Clever. A bit wild. *Troubled.*

And, for tonight at least, he was all hers.

'I don't want promises.' And strangely enough she discovered that she didn't. All she wanted was the man. Mac. And she'd take him on whatever terms she was offered, for as long as she could have him.

He searched her eyes for answers to questions he hadn't even asked and then bent his head and took her mouth. And she closed her eyes and moaned because his kiss was everything she'd imagined it would be and so much more.

The erotic stroke of his tongue, the nip of his teeth

and the brush of his strong fingers against her cheek. It was a gentle seduction, a prelude to something more—*a promise*...

Louisa started to shiver and instantly he lifted his head, his eyes glittering in the semi-darkness.

'You're cold.' His voice was rough. 'Let's get home.'

How did she tell him that she wasn't cold? That the tremors attacking her body had nothing to do with the temperature and everything to do with her reaction to him?

Or perhaps he understood that.

She saw his hard eyes gleam brightly before he unlocked the car and bundled her inside.

He drove quickly but carefully, his eyes fixed on the road in concentration, his profile hard and un-smiling.

What was he thinking?

It was snowing again and Mac flicked on the wind-screen wipers as huge white flakes raced towards them.

He headed for the coast road and Louisa squinted as headlights came towards them at speed. One min-ute the car was on the other side of the road and the next it was directly in their path.

Mac gave a vicious curse and swung the wheel hard, steering back again to pull the car out of a spin. It all happened so fast that Louisa didn't even have time to cry out.

Her stomach lurched with horror and she braced herself for the impact, but there was no sound and she realised that Mac had skilfully avoided a head-on collision.

He struggled to bring the car under control on the icy road, his hands tight on the wheel, his concentration absolute as he slowed his speed and controlled the skid.

Louisa closed her eyes and breathed out slowly.

It was all right.

And then she heard a sickening thud.

Mac brought the car to a halt at the side of the road, hit the switch for the hazard warning lights and turned towards her, his expression urgent. 'Are you hurt?' He switched off the ignition and an eerie silence descended on them. 'Louisa, are you OK?'

She looked down at herself and discovered that her hands were shaking. 'I'm fine.' *Pull yourself together.* 'Mac, they were driving like maniacs.'

His expression was grim. 'I know. The car's in the ditch.' He opened his door and unclipped his seat belt. 'Use my mobile. Call the emergency services. I'm going to see what I can do.'

It took her a moment to act. Her brain felt numb. Everything seemed to be happening in slow motion.

Then she glanced over her shoulder and saw the car in the ditch and Mac picking his way over the icy road towards it. Reality hit.

She reached for the phone and made the call, rubbing a hand across her forehead as she tried to give the emergency services their precise location.

Then she grabbed her coat around her and slithered across the road to join him, wishing that she was wearing something more sensible on her feet. Her shoes weren't designed to be anything other than decorative.

Her heart was racing and her palms were clammy,

partly as a reaction from their near miss but also in anticipation of what lay ahead. Despite the fact she'd worked in A and E for several years, she'd never attended the scene of an accident before.

Mac already had his head inside the driver's window and was talking to someone, the beam of his torch cutting through the darkness. The snow was falling heavily now and the temperature was dropping. 'Louisa.' His breath clouded the air as he glanced over her shoulder, his expression urgent. 'I need a stronger torch and some blankets. And the bag from my boot. Quickly.'

She stood frozen to the spot in horror, staring at the mangled wreckage of the car and the teenage boy in the driver's seat who was clearly seriously injured.

'Oh, God, they're kids, Mac,' she whispered. 'Just kids.'

'Old enough to drive a car,' Mac said steadily. 'I need that bag.'

Quickly she turned and scrambled back up the bank on shaking legs and slithered across the road to the car. She fumbled with the door, tugged it open and rummaged around in the boot until she found what he needed. Then she slithered back across the road and down the bank to the wreckage.

Mac had prised open the driver's door and was half inside the car, talking to one of the boys.

Louisa flicked on the torch and directed the beam towards him. 'I've got your bag.'

'Good girl.' He turned and took it from her, wedging it on the dashboard so that the interior of the car was illuminated. 'Right, this guy is unconscious and from the little I can see with this totally useless torch he has extensive bruising to his chest from the steering-wheel. He's got asymmetrical chest movement and a deviated trachea. I need to immobilise his neck and treat the pneumothorax.'

'What do you want me to do?'

'Go round to the passenger,' Mac ordered, adjusting the angle of the torch. 'He's conscious and talking but there's blood coming from somewhere and the light isn't good enough to see where.'

Louisa scrambled round the car and tugged at the door. 'It's stuck, Mac.'

'Pull harder.'

She gritted her teeth and tugged hard but the door was totally jammed. 'There's no getting in this way.'

'Well, I'm not moving the driver until we can support his spine. We're going to need the fire brigade. Which emergency service did you ask for?'

'All of them,' Louisa muttered, shifting her coat out of the way, 'just to be on the safe side.'

'Good girl.'

Louisa tried the rear door of the car. 'Mac, I could climb into the back seat—I might be able to get to him between the seats.'

'Go for it.' Mac was still dealing with the driver. 'But watch yourself.'

Louisa hitched her long dress up to her waist and slithered onto the back seat. The smell of alcohol hit her and she screwed up her face. *They'd been drinking.*

Reminding herself that it wasn't the right time to moralise, she focused on her patient. 'Hello. Everything is going to be fine.' Why did people say that, she wondered to herself, when clearly things were anything but fine? 'Can you tell me what hurts?'

'My arm.' The boy's voice was so weak it was barely audible. 'My arm is agony.'

'All right.' Louisa shifted her position and yanked at her dress as it caught in her heel. There was a tearing sound that made her wince. *So much for the dress.* 'I'm going to try and take a look at what's happening.'

Mac glanced across, his face barely visible in the shadows. 'Be careful. There's broken glass everywhere. Don't cut yourself.'

Louisa wondered how she was supposed to not cut herself when she had no room to manoeuvre and could barely see in the darkness.

She dragged on a pair of gloves, which she found in her pocket, ripped open some dressing pads from Mac's bag and then leaned forward to find where the bleeding was coming from. 'Mac.' Her voice shook slightly and she just hated herself for sounding so pathetic, 'There's blood everywhere—I can't get close enough to apply pressure.'

But the boy was cold, she could feel that much.

Without thinking, she struggled out of her coat and covered the injured passenger.

'Just do your best,' Mac said grimly. 'I'll be with you in a minute.'

Twisting her body slightly, Louisa managed to wriggle between the seats and move the teenager's sleeve. Blood spurted into the air. 'It's an artery.' She slammed a pad down on the pumping wound and felt her hands start to shake. 'He's hit an artery.'

Her fingers slithered and slipped on the wound and

she gritted her teeth and reached behind her for more pads with her free hand. To her relief, she could hear sirens and see flashing lights.

Thank goodness.

Mac vanished from his position by the driver and shouted up to the paramedics and the fire brigade.

Bright lights shone in her face and suddenly she could see properly.

'Get me a wide-bore cannula,' Mac was saying, and one of the paramedics was by his side, helping him to drain the pneumothorax.

After that it was a blur of activity.

Once Mac had stabilised the driver he moved to the other side of the car and helped Louisa, who was keeping the pressure on the wound, even though she could feel the bandages were already soaked.

With the minimum of fuss he inserted two wide-bore cannulae and started IV fluids.

Louisa's teeth were chattering and she could no longer feel her fingers. 'Shouldn't we just get him to hospital as fast as possible?'

'Yes.' Mac applied more pads and pressure to the arm. 'But while they're evacuating the driver he can be getting fluids. Time is crucial and he's lost a lot of blood.'

Relieved that her part in the rescue was over, Louisa wriggled out of the back of the car and stumbled up onto the bank.

One of the paramedics frowned at her. 'Are you OK, love?'

'No.' Mac's tone was short as he joined them, snow clinging to his coat. 'I should think she's in the early stages of hypothermia. I need to get her home before she freezes. She wasn't exactly dressed for the rigours of emergency care at the roadside.'

'We could take her in if you like.'

'Into A and E?' Louisa's voice was a squeak of horror. 'You're joking!'

She couldn't think of anything more embarrassing.

'I'll take her home,' Mac said roughly, watching as they loaded the casualties into the ambulance. 'Will you take it from here?'

'Certainly will.' The paramedic smiled. 'Josh on at the unit?'

Mac nodded, a ghost of a smile flickering across his handsome face. 'Tell him I'm sending him an early Christmas present.'

'Will do.' He secured the doors and walked round to the front.

At that moment the police drew up and Mac strode across to speak to them.

Louisa watched from a distance while Mac outlined what had happened, gesturing with his hand to show how the car had crossed onto the wrong side of the road.

The police asked him a number of questions and then Mac strode back across to her.

'Let's go.'

'Have they finished talking to you?'

'For now.'

'Good. Because I'm a bit cold.' She was shivering so hard she could barely speak and he cursed under his breath as he helped her across the road and into the car. He yanked open the door and then glanced over his shoulder, his gaze on the wreckage in the ditch. His stare was bleak and full of ghosts and Louisa frowned.

Was he thinking of his wife?

'Mac? Are you OK?'

He pulled himself together. 'Fine. Cover yourself with these.' He reached into the back of the car, thrust a couple of blankets onto her lap and added his own coat on top.

'You can't give me your coat,' she protested, but he ignored her and swung himself into the driver's seat.

'We'll be home in less than five minutes and then we'll warm you up.'

Louisa tried to stop her teeth chattering and wondered exactly what form the 'warming up' was going to take.

The romance of the evening was gone.

Now that the urgency of the situation had passed, reaction set in. With vivid clarity she remembered the headlights coming towards them—and Mac's swift avoiding action.

'Were they drunk, do you think? Do you think they were driving too fast? They almost hit us, Mac.'

If it hadn't been for his skilled driving, they would have had a head-on collision.

The thought made her shiver.

'The roads are icy.' His tone was flat, devoid of emotion. 'I suppose they just lost control of the car. The driving conditions are lethal and they're young, inexperienced.'

Unlike him. His skill behind the wheel had undoubtedly saved them from being part of the accident.

'Do you think they'll be OK?'

His gaze didn't shift from the road. 'Yes.'

Because of him. She felt her insides turn over. 'You were amazing and I was totally hopeless,' she muttered. 'I'm so sorry.'

He frowned, his hands firm on the wheel. 'You weren't hopeless.'

She huddled under the blankets. 'Yes, I was. I've never actually dealt with a situation like that before. I completely panicked.'

'It's perfectly normal to panic faced with those circumstances,' he said gently. 'It's very different from what we do on the unit.'

'I find it really scary,' she confessed. 'Being first on the scene, making decisions that could mean the difference between life and death. And through it all you're developing frostbite and you can't see a damn thing.'

Mac gave a short laugh. 'So you're not going to give up your day job and become a paramedic, then?'

'Well, they do at least have equipment,' she pointed out, and he nodded and swung the car into his driveway.

'I was waiting for you to invite them for Christmas. Along with the occupants of the car, the fire brigade and the police.' He leaned across and undid her seat belt, his expression slightly mocking. 'For once you were very restrained.'

'My jaw was frozen. I couldn't speak properly.'

His gaze drifted to her mouth. 'Then we'd better do something about that. Starting with a hot shower.'

CHAPTER EIGHT

THEY used his bathroom.

Louisa was shivering so much she could barely speak and Mac pushed her soaking wet coat off her shoulders with a rough exclamation. 'You're soaked through. Let's get this dress off.'

Louisa tried to smile but her teeth were chattering too much. 'I bet you use that line on all the girls.'

'Never before to one covered in blood and soaked through,' Mac assured her in a dry tone, sliding the zip down with brisk efficiency and reaching into the cubicle to turn on the shower. Jets of hot water hissed and steamed and Louisa stepped out of her torn, filthy dress, watching regretfully as it lay limply at her feet.

'I spent a lot of money on that. What a waste.'

'Never mind that now.' Mac adjusted the flow of the shower and jerked his head. 'Take your underwear off and get in the shower. We need to warm you up.'

She rolled her eyes, her teeth still chattering. 'You have a strange line in seduction.'

'Louisa!' His tone was exasperated. 'I'm trying to stop you freezing to death!'

'Well, I can't undress with you watching me,' she shot back, scraping her sodden hair out of her eyes with a shaking hand. 'Turn your back.'

Mac exhaled slowly, his eyes suddenly very dark. 'I'm a doctor.'

'You're also a man, Mac!' And a man she wanted

so much she ached for his touch. But not like this. Not when she was so vulnerable. She felt shy, awkward. 'I'm an old-fashioned girl! I can't undress with you watching!'

His jaw hardened and his eyes clashed with hers for a long moment. Then he muttered something under his breath and turned round as she'd instructed. 'Just get in the shower,' he growled, running a hand over the back of his neck, 'or I'll be taking you back to A and E and I've had enough of the place for one day.'

She undid her bra, stepped out of her panties and walked into the shower, her body still shuddering with the cold. Hot needles of water stung her freezing flesh and she gasped.

'Are you all right?' He turned and she suddenly realised that he was soaked through, too, and she hadn't even noticed. His dark hair was flattened to his head and his previously pristine dinner suit clung to his broad shoulders.

His jaw was rough and dark and his eyes were restless. He looked dishevelled, more than a little disreputable and all the man she'd ever wanted.

She felt a sudden jolt and desire overwhelmed shyness with the force of a tidal wave.

'You need a shower, too.' Gradually her body was warming up and the shivers lessened.

'I'll live.'

'Mac.' Her voice was pure female invitation and his eyes locked with hers. Something passed between them. She saw the heat flash in his eyes, registered the sudden tension in his broad shoulders. Then he lifted his hands and slowly, deliberately, unbuttoned his shirt.

Her heart beat a hectic rhythm and her body started to shiver again, but this time it was nothing to do with the cold.

His eyes still on hers, he let the shirt slip off his shoulders and dealt with his trousers.

He was all hard muscle and masculine perfection and Louisa felt her legs weaken. When he stepped into the cubicle with her, she closed her eyes.

The first purposeful slide of his hand down her bare back made her gasp with anticipation. Her whole body throbbed with awareness, her senses sang and excitement coiled and uncoiled low in her pelvis.

'Are you warming up yet?' His voice was husky and sexy and reflected everything that was happening between them.

Her eyes opened and locked on his.

'Oh, yes.' She didn't even question what she was doing. *There was nothing to question.*

The tension that had been building for days hovered between them and then it tightened and snapped.

His mouth came down on hers with ruthless intent, taking, ravaging, rough in his hunger for her. She didn't mind. She welcomed the force that consumed them both. She wouldn't have wanted less.

And she'd always known that Mac was a man who wouldn't hold back. A man whose passions ran deep.

Her pulse hammering, she dug her fingers in his sleek flesh, loving the hardness, the maleness, the contrast to her own body. Her mouth opened under his and she gave back willingly, welcoming his lead, matching his fierce passion.

He pressed her back against the tiled wall, trapping her with his body. He was all hard strength and masculinity and she slid her hands over the smooth muscle of his shoulders, grasping, seeking, wanting more.

She felt the nip of his teeth on her neck and then the brush of his mouth as it trailed downwards, and then his mouth closed over the tip of one breast, sucking her into darkness and another world. Heat sizzled and burned deep inside her and she cried out her need and pressed against him. Her eyes closed, her soft lips parted and her fingers tangled in his sleek hair as she strained against him.

'Louisa.' The rough sound of her name on his lips was somewhere between a curse and a promise and his strong hands skimmed down her body until he found what he wanted.

And he took.

With a skilled touch he learned and discovered, building the level of intimacy until she could no longer breathe properly, until her body was a shivering, seething mass of uncontrollable need.

She flung back her head and gasped his name in a plea that came perilously close to begging.

His hands were hard on her hips as he lifted her, his breathing harsh, his eyes darkened by a passion stronger than both of them.

With swift, sure movements he positioned her, supporting her easily, and then he thrust hard, taking her with almost fierce desperation, driven by the wildness that was consuming both of them.

She cried out in shock at his first invasion, her fingers biting into the hard muscle of his shoulders as her body adjusted to the pulsing pressure of his. She felt him pause, his breathing harsh as he struggled to drag himself back from the brink of insanity, and then she felt the heat curl over her again and brought her mouth down on his.

She didn't want him to stop.

She felt his hesitation, the briefest flicker of indecision, and then he drove into her again, but this time his movements were more controlled. She struggled to move her hips, to match his movements, but in this position she felt helpless and totally under his control. She felt the primitive rhythm, the heated, pulsing force of masculine possession and felt the frantic, desperate response of her own body.

Desire ripped through her and she gasped at the intensity of that sensation, so all-consuming, so primitive. Why had she ever thought that desire could be controlled? She could no more control what was happening than she could halt wind or rain.

His rough jaw scraped against hers and he took her cries into his mouth, his mouth demanding that she give still more. And she gave willingly. All of herself to this man. *Her man.* It was wild and crazy and totally out of control, and everything swirled and tangled until sensation exploded inside her with frightening intensity. Her body gripped his and he groaned her name before she felt the hot, liquid force of his own climax.

She clung to him with an almost fierce desperation as if he were the only thing standing between her and insanity, waiting for her senses to settle.

Mac continued to hold her, his breathing harsh and unsteady, his heart pounding against the rapid beat of hers as he struggled to regain control.

Then he withdrew slowly and lowered her, but still his hands held her, as if he knew by instinct that to release her now would have her collapsing at his feet.

Without speaking he reached out a hand and cut the flow of water.

Silence throbbed between them.

Louisa kept her eyes closed as she tried to regain some sort of composure. What were you supposed to say to a man after something so amazing?

She felt stunned. Shocked. *Exhilarated.*

'Louisa?' His voice was low and rough and then she felt the soft warmth of a towel being wrapped around her. He lifted her in his arms and carried her through to the bedroom. 'You should have told me.'

'Told you what?'

He deposited her gently in the middle of the bed and his eyes glittered in the semi-darkness. 'That it was your first time. I had no idea...'

'You didn't need to know.' Away from the warmth of the shower and the heat of his body, she started to shiver.

With a soft curse he removed the damp towel and, after the slightest hesitation, joined her in the bed.

He curved her against the warmth of his body and reached down to cover them both with the duvet. 'I wish you'd told me.'

Warmth spread through her.

She slid an arm over his chest, endlessly fascinated by the differences between them. He was hard to her soft. *Male to her female.* 'What difference would it have made?'

He tightened his hold and released a long breath. 'Well, for a start I would have been gentle.'

She pressed her mouth to his flesh. 'I didn't want you to be gentle.' She'd wanted all that he was. The man she knew him to be.

'Louisa—'

'Mac.' She lifted her head and her long hair trailed over his bare chest. 'Stop worrying. I'm fine.' She gave a womanly smile and her eyes dropped to his mouth. 'In fact, I'm more than fine.'

She felt his hesitation and decided that this time it was up to her to take the lead. Her body sliding over his, she lowered her mouth to his, teasing his lower lip with her tongue, offering him her kiss.

He watched her from under lowered lids, his expression unreadable, and for a long, pulsing moment she thought he might reject her. Then he muttered something against her mouth and his hands came up to trap her head as he gave her the response she'd been hoping for.

This time his kiss was slower and he explored every part of her mouth, controlling the pace, stoking the heat.

Louisa moaned against his lips as the now familiar burn low in her pelvis started to build.

She'd never met a man who could kiss like Mac. The moment he touched his lips to hers she could feel the effects through her whole body.

His kiss drove her pulse rate into a wild sprint and she straddled him, but he lifted his hands and caught her writhing hips.

'Not yet. This time we do it differently.' His voice was husky as he rolled her on her back and stroked a leisurely hand down her quivering, aching body. 'This time we take our time.'

The wild burning in her pelvis was so intense that she shifted against the sheets, desperate to ease the throbbing, burning ache that had become the entire focus of her being.

He held her down, refusing to allow her the satisfaction she craved until he was ready, using his mouth and fingers to drive her wild.

Louisa couldn't believe the intimacies she allowed him or those she gave in return, and when he finally rose over her she was sobbing his name and quivering in anticipation, the excitement almost intolerable.

He raised her hips and paused, his eyes dark as he gazed down at her, watching her reaction.

'Mac…please…' She was almost begging, beside herself with a need that she didn't recognise, and he lowered his head and took her mouth, his kiss as intimate as the rest of his touch.

This time he entered her slowly, the controlled thrust of his hips as erotic as it was gentle.

How did he know? she wondered dimly.

How did he know just how to move, just how to hold her so that both their bodies achieved the maximum response?

She curled her legs around him and arched her hips, drawing him deeper, urging him on.

The rhythm was slow and easy but the connection between them was no less intense for the lack of pace. This time the passion was dark and molten, twining itself around both of them, drawing them deeper and deeper.

And Louisa clung to him, her body matching his demands with demands of her own, discovering all that her body could do. *Could feel.*

'Mac, Mac.' She cried out his name and he dragged a hand into her hair, holding her head so that she was forced to look at him.

And the connection was complete.

She drowned in his dark eyes and felt her body convulse in an explosion of white light.

She heard his harsh groan and then her climax consumed her, shattering control and rational thought, and she lost herself completely in the experience that was loving Mac.

Breathless and weakened, she clung to him, her fingers holding onto his sleek flesh as both of them struggled to descend back into reality.

Then he shifted his weight and rolled onto his back, taking her with him.

So this was what it felt like to be in love.

She lay still for a moment, savouring the fact that it had finally happened. That she'd finally met the man of her dreams. And then she closed her eyes and succumbed to the delicious lethargy that spread through her entire body.

Flattened and exhausted by the depth of her own response, Louisa curled herself around him and slept like a child.

Mac poured coffee, choosing to drink it strong and black.

He needed the caffeine hit.

The overnight snowfall had transformed the world into a festive wonderland, and from the large windows in the kitchen he could see a family walking on the beach, throwing snowballs and clowning about.

He sipped the scalding brew, trying to chase away

the clouds that fogged his brain. Overnight the world seemed different and the reason for that was lying upstairs in his bed.

It had taken all his will-power to leave her sleeping.

Part of him had wanted to wake her from sleep in the oldest way known to man. But the other part of him—*the part of him he'd lived with since Melissa's death*—had known that he had to walk away.

While he still could.

He drained the coffee and poured another cup, wondering what had happened to his self-control. He'd always considered himself to be a disciplined man. Hell, it wasn't as if he hadn't been confronted by temptation before. He had, on many an occasion. And each time he'd had no trouble resisting.

It had been the accident. *The sudden surge of adrenaline that had needed to find a release.*

The accident and Louisa herself.

He swore under his breath, forced to acknowledge that Louisa, with her softness and her infectious personality, had sneaked under his skin despite all his efforts to keep her at a distance.

A sound in the doorway made him turn and he felt as though he'd been thumped in the gut.

'Hi.' Her hair was soft and tousled from sleep and wild love-making, her soft mouth bruised from his attentions. The physical evidence of his own lack of control made his mouth tighten in a grim line.

The knowledge that he'd been rougher than he should have been just added to his list of crimes.

'Are you planning to share that coffee?'

He reached for the jug and poured her a cup. 'We need to talk.'

'Right. That sounds ominous.' She stayed in the doorway, her eyes wary, and he mentally cursed his lack of self-control. Why the hell had he succumbed to temptation?

Then his gaze drifted to her brown eyes and he saw kindness, warmth and a memory of the passion he'd awakened the previous night.

And suddenly he knew exactly why he'd succumbed.

She was all woman. In every sense of the word.

'Stop panicking, Mac.' Her tone was soft as she stepped forward and took the cup he was still clutching in his hand. 'If this is the point where you feel obliged to point out that last night was a mistake, you're wasting your breath. It wasn't a mistake and there's no way you'll convince me that it was.'

He watched while she pulled out a chair and settled herself comfortably, her coffee on the table in front of her.

'I can't give you what you need.' He put his empty mug down on the table and looked at her warily, braced for her reaction.

Her dark lashes lowered slightly and her mouth curved into a half-smile that took him out at the knees. 'You were pretty good at giving me what I needed last night.' It was the voice of a seductress, smoky and soft, and it made him want to surrender on the spot.

'Louisa, you were a virgin.' He said it to remind himself as much as her. She wasn't the sort of woman who went into for casual relationships. Hadn't Josh told him that right at the beginning?

She frowned. 'What's that got to do with any-thing?'

'A lot. You've got this dream in your head. You've had it there since you were a child.' He sucked in a breath and forced himself to say the words. 'I can't be that dream.'

He was lousy at relationships.

'You're frightened because I said I wanted five kids.' She spooned sugar into her coffee. 'Relax. I'll settle for four, providing at least one of them is a girl.'

'This isn't a joke.'

She sighed and ran a hand through her tangled hair, visibly tired. 'No, but you are taking it all much too seriously. We had an amazing night. Let's leave it at that.'

'Is that what you want?'

'You want me to tell you what I want?' She spread her hands. 'All right, let's be totally honest. I love you, Mac. Very much. And to be honest, that comes as a bit of a shock to me because you're not the sort of man I thought I'd eventually fall for.'

He couldn't have been more shocked if she'd punched him in the jaw. 'You don't love me, Louisa.'

She reached for her coffee. 'Yes, I do.' Her tone was matter-of-fact. 'Weird, isn't it?'

She loved him?

He gritted his teeth. 'Louisa, you can't love me. You're mistaking sex for love. Believe me, it's easily done.'

'Maybe for some people.' She took a sip of coffee. 'But not for me.'

He gritted his teeth. 'I was your first lover.'

'And you were amazing,' she said softly. 'I feel

sorry for every woman in the world who didn't go to sleep curled around you last night.'

He closed his eyes. 'You don't know me. You don't know the man I am.'

'Well, I'm trying,' she said lightly, 'although it's pretty hard because you don't leave that many clues lying around, do you? You shut every piece of yourself away and don't let anyone in. You scare everyone away because you pretend to be so remote and chilly. But that isn't the way you are, is it? Not really. I've seen you with patients. I've seen you with your brother. You're capable of great warmth and kindness.'

'I don't do relationships, Louisa.' He had to be honest with her even though he knew he'd be hurting her. 'Not any more.'

There was a long silence.

Then she gave a brave smile. 'No.' Her tone was wistful. 'Of course you don't. I understand.'

No, she didn't. She didn't understand anything.

For a brief, frustrating moment Mac wanted to smash his fist into the wall.

'Louisa—'

'Oh, no!' She stood up suddenly, almost tipping the chair in the process, her eyes sliding round the kitchen.

He frowned. *Now what?* 'What's the matter?'

'Where's Hopeful?' She raked tangled dark curls out of her eyes, her expression anxious as she searched under the table and behind the curtains. 'We left him in here last night. I thought we shut the door.'

Mac thought for a moment and then groaned. 'He rushed past me when I opened the door this morning.'

He hadn't been concentrating. He'd other things on his mind.

Like the way she'd given all of herself to him. No holding back.

'I hope he hasn't been up to mischief.' She hurried out of the kitchen and Mac followed her, biting his lip to prevent himself from pointing out that Hopeful's entire life consisted of mischief.

She saw the best in everyone. Even the dog.

They found Hopeful in the sitting room, coughing up pieces of coloured paper over the polished floor, the Christmas tree lying full length across the room.

'Oh, no, he's knocked the tree over.' In a second she was on her knees by the dog. 'Did you have a fright, darling? Are you hurt?'

Mac looked at the debris over his sitting room and shook his head in disbelief. 'Nothing would hurt that dog,' he said dryly. 'He's indestructible.'

'He's eaten something, Mac.' Louisa picked up some bits of shiny paper and then glanced at the tree. 'He's eaten the chocolate decorations. Including the paper.'

'Not very discriminating, then.'

Louisa stuck her fingers in the dog's mouth. 'Spit it out, Hopeful,' she urged. 'Come on, darling, you can't eat that.'

Mac looked at the mess on his floor. 'I think he has already spat it out. All over my living room.'

Louisa didn't even look up. 'We need to take him to the vet again. All that paper might upset his insides.'

'My credit card hasn't recovered from the last visit.'

'Don't joke.' Louisa scrambled to her feet, dragging Hopeful with her. 'Let's get him in the car. Quick, Mac.'

'Louisa.' Mac tried to keep his tone patient, 'the dog will be fine. Whatever he's swallowed will come out again. That dog looks totally healthy. Just a little sick from too much chocolate.'

She bit her lip, her arms still wrapped round the dog. 'You don't know that. You're not a vet.'

Realising that nothing short of a big bill was going to reassure her, Mac gave a sigh and reached for his coat.

'All right, we'll go. But you'd better put some clothes on or you'll shock the vet.'

CHAPTER NINE

THE vet was suitably reassuring. 'Don't give him any more chocolate,' he said as he finished examining Hopeful, 'and don't worry about the paper. It will work its way out.'

'Probably over my carpets,' Mac said wearily as he proffered his credit card again.

They walked back to the car, leading a chastened Hopeful.

'There, darling,' Louisa said gently, 'you sit in the back.'

'And if you're sick in my car, you're going back in the ditch,' Mac muttered, and Louisa smiled at him.

'I know you don't mean that.'

Mac slid into the driver's seat next to her. 'Louisa, that dog has cost me a fortune! Vet's bills are outrageous. Do you realise how much I just paid him for the privilege of being told not to give him any more chocolate? Chocolate that I didn't want him to eat in the first place.'

Louisa chuckled. The truth was she was grateful to Hopeful for offering a distraction.

When she'd woken that morning and found Mac gone, she'd felt as though she'd been showered with cold water. Nothing had prepared her for waking up alone.

The night they'd spent together had been intense, frantic, passionate and totally honest.

He'd held nothing back from her. *And she'd held nothing back from him.*

So she hadn't expected the chill she'd experienced when she'd walked into the kitchen.

It was like going from the tropics to the Arctic without a suitable change of clothes.

How could he be prepared to walk away from what they'd shared? How could he pretend that it had meant nothing?

Louisa bit her lip and stared out of the window. Anything rather than look at him. It was time to accept some truths. She had to accept that, for Mac, no one would ever replace his wife. Clearly she had left a gap that no one could ever fill, she thought miserably, watching as the snowy countryside flashed past.

And one night of passion, however breathtaking, wasn't going to change that.

She could force him to accept people into his life, but she couldn't force him to accept her into his heart.

Christmas Eve turned out to be the busiest day of the year in the A and E department.

Louisa found herself working alongside Josh as they struggled to cope with the steady influx of patients.

'Fifty-year-old man coming in with chest pain,' she called out to him as she replaced the receiver of the ambulance hotline. 'They'll be here in five minutes. Shall I see if there's room in Resus?'

Josh shook his head. 'Mac's already in there with two patients and there's an RTA coming in—the guy will be safer in one of the side rooms where the equipment hasn't been stripped. Let's get an ECG ready and prepare some drugs. And run through an IV.'

Louisa nodded, seeing the sense in what he was saying. They were still working on two patients in Resus and they hadn't yet had time to restock the equipment.

'So much for spending the day eating mince pies and singing Christmas carols,' she said dryly, and Josh looked at her.

'Are you all right? You look tired.'

She was exhausted. *Thanks to the bedroom skills of his brother.*

'I'm fine.'

Josh cast her a speculative glance. 'You're far from fine. What's happened?'

Louisa felt the colour seep into her cheeks and Josh gave a sigh.

'OK, I know that look. You'd better tell me everything.'

'There's nothing to tell.' She gave a tiny shrug. 'Your brother is so in love with his wife that he can't see another woman and perhaps he never will.'

'Is that what he told you?' Josh stared at her in shock and then gave a little shake of his head. 'No, Louisa, that isn't—'

The shriek of a siren interrupted them and Louisa glanced towards the doorway, pleased for the excuse to change the subject. She didn't really want to talk about it. The discovery that she'd finally fallen in love with a man who couldn't love her back left her hollow inside. She'd waited so long to meet a man she knew she could be happy with, could make a family with. 'We can't talk about this now. That's our patient. I'll get the side room ready.' She gathered together all the things she anticipated that they'd need just as the ambulance arrived.

She recognised the paramedic from the accident the night before. 'Hi.'

His face brightened as he recognised her. 'Well, if it isn't our little heroine. Those kids are doing really well, thanks to you and Mac.' He pushed the stretcher alongside the trolley. 'This is Tom Parker. He was at his firm's Christmas party when he started getting central chest pains radiating down the arm.'

'It's just indigestion,' the man groaned, screwing up his face as the pain hit again. 'Too many sausage rolls. And I should never have danced with the girl from Accounts.'

'Sounds like a good party,' Josh drawled. 'We just need to transfer you onto our trolley and then we can take a look at you.'

Louisa and the paramedics helped the man across onto the A and E trolley. 'Have you ever had these pains before?'

Her eyes scanned the patient, noticing that he was very pale and sweaty. Alarm bells rang in her head. This had nothing to do with sausage rolls.

She glanced at Josh. 'Right with you,' he said softly, as he reached for a cannula. 'We've called the coronary care team. They're on their way. Give him a puff of GTN spray, Louisa,' he ordered as he slid the cannula into the vein. Then his blue eyes lifted to hers. 'And when we're done here, you and I need to have a talk.'

What was there to talk about?

She was in love with his brother and talking about

it wasn't going to change the facts. That he didn't love her.

Louisa checked the patient's observations while Josh carried out his examination and checked the ECG trace.

'He has ST elevation and pathological Q waves,' he muttered, his eyes fixed on the trace. He turned to the SHO who was working with him. 'Let's get a line in, take bloods for urgent U and E, glucose, CK, FBC and baseline cholesterol. And let's give him something for the pain. Louisa?'

Louisa handed him a syringe of morphine and cyclizine for sickness. 'Is there anyone you'd like me to phone, Tom?' She checked his blood-pressure reading again. 'Is your family expecting you home?'

He nodded, his face contorted with the pain. 'My wife. But not until later. I was expecting to stay at the party until mid-afternoon. I left the car at home. She was going to pick me up.'

'Sensible man,' Louisa said, thinking of the two teenagers. 'I'll call her,' she promised. 'Do you have a number?'

At that moment the coronary care team arrived and Louisa wrote down the number that Tom gave her and made the call, choosing her words carefully so that she didn't worry his wife.

Tom was transferred quickly to Coronary Care and Louisa found herself helping out in the treatment room, dressing the arm of a child who had cut herself.

'Her brother threw a snowball and it must have had a stone in it,' the mother told her helplessly, looking completely fraught. 'Can you imagine? For the first time in years it snows and we all think we're going to have a fairy-tale Christmas and here we are in A and E! We were supposed to be sitting by the fire, watching the repeats on the television and arguing.'

Louisa laughed. 'Isn't that life, though? It never quite works out the way you expect.'

Hers certainly didn't.

She finished bandaging the child's arm and wished her concentration was better. *All she could think about was Mac.*

She'd arrived just for Christmas and suddenly all she wanted to do was stay for ever.

Her hands stilled on the bandage and for a moment her need for him was so severe that she could hardly breathe. Was this what he'd felt for Melissa? If so, no wonder he couldn't move on. No wonder he couldn't fully give himself to anyone else. She couldn't imagine ever having this depth of feeling again.

He was right when he said that she wanted happy ever after. It was all she'd ever wanted—with the right man. But sadly Mac didn't think he was the right man.

'Nurse?' The mother was watching her closely. 'Are you all right?'

Louisa made a supreme effort and managed a smile. 'I'm fine, thanks. Just a little tired. We've been terribly busy. A white Christmas is pretty but it creates havoc in A and E. Come back in three days to have the dressing changed. And have a lovely Christmas.'

'Can we go home now?' The little girl looked at her, her eyes shining with excitement. 'Santa is coming tonight. I have to be asleep or he doesn't come.'

Louisa felt her heart twist. 'That's right. So you do.' She brushed the child's hair out of her eyes. 'Did you write him a letter?'

The little girl nodded her head solemnly. 'I asked for a doll. The one that wets her nappy and drinks from a bottle.'

Louisa nodded. 'Sounds great.'

She watched them go with a wistful expression on her face, wondering whether she'd ever know what it was like to be part of a family.

It had been her dream for as long as she could remember.

And it looked as though that was where it was going to stay. *In her dreams.*

Mother and child left just as Mac put his head round the door. 'There you are. I've been looking for you.'

Her heart leapt and danced in her chest and suddenly she felt light-headed. 'Did you need me for something?'

He gave a brief nod. 'A woman just wrapped her car round a tree. She'll be here in five minutes. I need the trauma team in Resus.' He looked drawn and tired. 'Louisa, will you bleep the surgeons and make arrangements for a CT scan just in case...?'

Work.

With him it was always work.

And he didn't need her for anything except his trauma team.

She gave a nod and turned her back for a moment to hide the pain in her eyes. 'I'll be there in just a moment.' She tipped the debris from the dressing into the bin, keeping her back to him until she heard the door swing shut behind him. Then she turned her head and glanced towards the place he'd been standing, her eyes glistening with tears.

'You don't need me for anything, Mac Sullivan,' she said softly. 'Nothing at all.'

The woman was in bad shape.

'She's local and her husband is on the way in.' The paramedics transferred her across to the trolley and everyone swung into action.

From the start, Mac was white-faced and tense. 'Hannah, start the clock. Get a central line in but hold fluids until we know where she's bleeding from. She has distended neck veins.'

Josh administered oxygen. 'You think she has a cardiac tamponade?'

'I don't know.' Mac's face was grim. 'And until I know I'm not going to give indiscriminate fluid replacement. The aim is to restore circulatory status to the point of critical organ perfusion. If we raise arterial and intracardiac pressures we could cause fatal haemorrhage. Let's do a chest X-ray and a FAST examination.'

Hannah finished cutting off the patient's clothes. 'But this was blunt injury. Isn't cardiac tamponade usually a result of penetrating injury? Stabbings and so forth?'

'Usually but not always.'

Louisa let her gaze slip to Mac. He didn't take his eyes off his patient. He was constantly monitoring, examining, looking for minute changes that might give clues as to the patient's condition.

He was a very talented doctor.

Now he was listening to the patient's heart, a frown on his handsome face. 'Can we keep the noise down, folks?' he growled, his eyes shut as he tried to concentrate. Moments later he ripped the stethoscope out of his ears. 'Muffled heart sounds and hypotension. I'm guessing she has cardiac tamponade. Let's do a scan. Are those X-rays ready?'

Sue put the films into the light box and Mac studied them carefully.

'Her pressure is falling,' Josh murmured, and Mac nodded as he scanned the patient.

Louisa watched as he placed the transducer just to the left of the xiphisternum and angled upwards under the coastal margin.

'I haven't seen that done before.'

Mac had his eyes on the screen. 'It's just an ultrasound that you can perform by the bedside.' He moved the transducer. 'Helps to identify intra-peritoneal haemorrhage or, in this case, pericardial tamponade.'

Josh looked at his brother. 'Her pressure is still falling.'

'She's not responding. Hannah, emergency bleep the cardiothoracic surgeons and let's attach the patient to an ECG. We're going to have to do an emergency pericardiocentesis—I want to see if I can draw some blood from the pericardial space. Louisa—get me a pack. Let's move, everyone. I won't lose her.'

There was something in his tone that made Louisa glance at his face. It was a mask, not one flicker of emotion showing on his features. She caught Josh's eye and he gave a brief shake of his head, indicating that she shouldn't interfere.

Reminding herself that she had a job to do, Louisa quickly grabbed the equipment he needed while Mac scrubbed and donned gloves and an apron.

He prepared the skin surgically and then held out a hand. 'Local anaesthetic—and then I'm going to need a wide-bore, plastic-sheathed needle.'

Louisa handed him the syringe and watched while he infiltrated the area and then inserted the needle. As the needle advanced Mac aspirated. 'This doesn't always work,' he murmured for the benefit of the more junior doctors who were watching in awed silence. 'In about a quarter of cases the blood around the pericardium has clotted and it isn't possible to aspirate.'

His eyes flickering to the ECG and then back to the syringe as it filled with blood. 'But in this case that hasn't happened. She's going to need a surgical exploration.'

'Her pressure is still falling,' Josh said, his eyes on the monitors, and Mac's mouth tightened.

'Someone get the surgeons up here *now*!'

His tone was harsh and unusually impatient, and Louisa knew that to Mac this case had become personal.

He was thinking of his wife.

'Her husband is still in the relatives' room,' Josh said wearily, after they'd handed the patient over to the cardiothoracic team and transferred her to Theatre. 'Do you want me to talk to him?'

Mac breathed out slowly and shook his head. 'No, I'll go and talk to him. But thanks.' He gave a wintry smile as he ripped off his gloves and dropped them in the bin. 'Louisa, will you come with me?'

They walked in silence to the relatives' room and Louisa felt Mac's tension grow with every step.

She could almost feel his pain.

Was he remembering another winter's evening when he'd been the one waiting to hear news?

Suddenly it didn't seem right that he was the one to do this, and she put a hand on his arm and stopped him. 'Wait.' Her tone was soft, and she pulled him to one side, conscious of the other members of staff hurrying past. 'You don't have to do this, Mac. Josh could do it. Or one of the others.'

He frowned. 'I'm fine.'

'You're not fine, Mac. I can see that you're—'

'Louisa, I'm fine.' He moved his arm, dislodging her hand, as cold and remote as she'd ever seen him. 'I need to do this. I was the one with the patient in Resus. It's my job.'

She opened her mouth to point out that Josh had been in Resus, too, but he was already striding down the corridor.

She gave a frustrated sigh and hurried after him.

The woman's husband was slumped in an armchair, his head in his hands. As the door opened he lifted his head and looked at them.

Louisa could almost taste his fear.

He breathed out slowly, his eyes reddened and his face tormented. 'Will she live?'

Mac ran a hand over the back of his neck, the tension visible in every angle of his handsome face. 'At the moment she's stable but it's too early to be sure that she's out of the woods. Her injuries were severe,' he said quietly. 'We've taken her to Theatre so that the surgeons can take a proper look at her chest.

We're doing everything we can and the surgeon is excellent. The best in the country.'

The husband let out a long breath. 'You think she might die?'

Mac took a moment to answer. 'I hope not,' he said finally, his tone gruff. 'I truly hope not. We'll keep you informed every step of the way.'

He was as good as his word.

He stayed at the hospital until the woman was out of Theatre and stable in ITU. Then he spent more time talking to her husband and the surgeon.

'Go home, Mac,' Hannah urged. 'You should have been off duty hours ago. You must be dropping.'

'I didn't want to leave until I knew what had happened in Theatre,' he said heavily, and Hannah glanced at Louisa.

She hadn't wanted to leave until she knew that Mac was all right. Which was ridiculous, she told herself firmly, because he didn't need comfort from her. He didn't need comfort from anyone.

His handsome face was shuttered. Blocking everyone out. No trace of emotion visible.

Louisa sighed.

Undoubtedly he was thinking of his wife.

Was this really the same man who had lost himself in her arms the night before?

'It's Christmas Eve,' Hannah reminded them, her tone exasperated as she waved a hand towards the massive tree that stood in the waiting room. 'You're supposed to be off duty and at home. Go and enjoy yourselves.'

'Yes.' Unsmiling, his hard features strained, Mac gave them a brief nod and walked towards his office.

'There goes a troubled man,' Hannah said softly, and Louisa nodded.

Thanks to Rick, her car was working again and she had her own transport home.

But would he want her company?

Something told her that the magic of last night was well and truly over.

She found him sitting in the darkness of the living room, his eyes closed, his legs stretched out in front of him.

The remains of a fire still flickered in the hearth but the room had a distinct chill about it.

Louisa hesitated in the doorway, her eyes adjusting to the gloom. There was something about the stillness of his body that suggested that he didn't want to be disturbed. But she couldn't walk away. His pain was like a living force, so powerful that she could feel it.

'Mac?'

For a moment he didn't answer and then his eyes opened and she saw the desolation and emptiness.

'Go to bed, Louisa.' His voice was gruff and she bit her lip.

'Not until I know you're all right.'

His eyes glittered hard in the darkness. 'You can't fix everything.'

'Neither can you.' She stepped forward into the room, fearing rejection and yet unable to leave him alone. 'You did everything you could, Mac. More than most would have done and she's holding her own. I just rang ITU to check.'

There was a long silence.

'Did you see his face?' He spoke slowly, almost talking to himself. 'It was like looking at myself in the mirror. A couple of years ago, I was in his shoes. Standing in the relatives' room, waiting for someone to come and tell me what the hell was happening to my wife.'

Hardly daring to breathe, Louisa tiptoed into the room. There was a long silence and she sat down timidly on the sofa next to him, braced for rejection.

'Do you want to talk about it?'

'No.' Mac closed his eyes and rested his head against the back of the sofa. 'Or maybe I do. I don't know. I've never tried it before. It was all too complicated.'

Louisa relaxed slightly, relieved that he hadn't sent her away. 'Is it so complicated just to say how you feel?'

He looked at her. 'It is when how you feel isn't the way people expect you to feel.'

She sat still. 'How did you feel, Mac?'

He closed his eyes. 'Angry. Frustrated. Let down.'

'It's normal to feel angry when people die.'

'That's what everyone told me. It's fine, they said, all part of the normal grieving process.' He gave a harsh laugh. 'They didn't have a bloody clue.' He looked at her. 'She was nothing like you. She wouldn't have been sitting there now, waiting patiently for me to talk. She would have been tapping her high-heeled shoes on the floor and glancing at her watch. For Melissa everything was measured in time. Billable hours.'

Louisa watched him. 'Tell me what she was like.'

'Melissa?' He dropped his head back against the sofa. 'She was driven. Wildly ambitious, political and totally focused on where she was going and how she was going to get there.'

'She was a doctor?'

Mac shook his head. 'A lawyer. She worked for a big, fancy firm in London and I met her when I was doing a stint for one of the London teaching hospitals. We got married. End of story.'

Except it wasn't the end of the story, Louisa mused. Any fool could see that.

He had so many emotions that he'd locked away.

'So you moved down here once you were married?'

'In a manner of speaking. There were firms down here that would have given her a partnership but she wasn't interested. She carried on working in London during the week and travelled here at weekends.'

Louisa hid her surprise. 'That's quite a journey.' Even with good roads that was a journey of at least five hours. 'You must have been very much in love.'

Mac made a noise that was somewhere between a groan and a laugh. 'Louisa, you are so innocent!' He turned his head towards her, his eyes tired and more than a little cynical. 'Such a romantic. I hate to dis-illusion you but my marriage was anything but a fairy-tale.'

She sat still, everything suddenly falling into place. 'You weren't in love with her?'

'At the beginning. Maybe.' He shrugged. 'Or maybe we weren't. We had a passionate relationship and I think we both confused that with love. But we didn't want the same things.'

'What did you want, Mac?' She hardly dared ask the question.

'I suppose I was pretty naïve, too,' he said gruffly. 'I thought we could both enjoy our careers until the time came when we were ready to start a family together. But Melissa didn't want that. Perhaps she never did. She was only interested in her career. In the next case. The adulation. She was seduced by her own success.'

'There are plenty of couples who both manage to have careers,' Louisa said softly, and Mac gave a bitter laugh.

'But generally they at least live in the same county. Melissa never had any intention of leaving London. She had to be at the heart of the action. A law firm outside the city was her idea of hell.'

'And you would never have left Cornwall because it's so much a part of who you are,' Louisa said softly, remembering how he content he seemed whenever he was at the beach or in the sea.

He gave her a curious look. 'I don't think Melissa ever understood that. Or maybe at the end she did.'

'What happened?'

He paused briefly. 'The night she died we'd been out for dinner.' His voice was flat and totally devoid of emotion. 'We both knew we needed to rethink our life together. I asked her to take a break from her job so that we could spend some time together...' He paused, his gaze fixed on the dying flame of the fire. 'She told me she'd met someone else and asked me for a divorce.'

Louisa felt something twist inside her. 'Oh, Mac...'

'Don't feel sorry for me.' He gave a harsh laugh.

'I felt nothing but relief. Relief that our farce of a marriage was finally to be over, and with the minimum fuss and bother. I sat there thinking that it was a good job that we'd never found the time to have children. It made everything so much simpler. Or it should have done. We would have told people straight away that weekend and that would have been the end of it, but she hit ice on her way back to London.'

Louisa swallowed. What had Melissa been thinking that night? Had she been upset that she'd finally ended the marriage? Not concentrating on the road? Or had she been driving too fast, eager to return to the arms of her lover?

'Afterwards her parents were distraught. They blamed me,' he said heavily, 'for expecting her to travel to me every weekend, for not putting enough effort into the marriage.'

'That's ridiculous,' Louisa said hotly. 'You had responsibilities at the hospital. You couldn't get away that easily.'

'Couldn't I?' His eyes glittered hard in the darkness. 'Or maybe I just didn't want to. Melissa always told me that I was terrible at relationships. She was right. I wasn't prepared to do what it took to make it work.'

'But maybe that was because you married the wrong person.'

He looked at her with a half-smile. 'You don't see bad in people, do you? I'm a selfish workaholic, Louisa. And you should stay away from me.'

She didn't want to stay away from him.

'You're a brilliant doctor,' she corrected him softly, 'and it's lucky for your patients you're a workaholic.

And I don't think you're selfish. I think you just know what you want. Unfortunately it wasn't the same thing that Melissa wanted. Did you tell her parents she was having an affair? That she wanted a divorce?'

'No.' His voice was hollow. 'It would have made things even worse. I didn't want their memory of her to be tainted.'

'I can understand that, I suppose.' Louisa frowned. 'But surely you must have told *someone*.'

'Just Josh. For everyone else it seemed kinder just to leave things as they were.'

'But not kinder for you.'

'What difference did it make to me? She was gone.'

'But you must have had so many feelings that you couldn't express,' Louisa said, her expression troubled. 'That night she died she also told you that she was having an affair and that she wanted a divorce. You must have felt totally betrayed.'

'What I really felt was that I didn't deserve the sympathy I was getting from everyone. I was a lousy husband.'

'So is that why you pushed everyone away? Because you felt you didn't deserve what they were offering?' She bit her lip. 'You're not to blame for her death, Mac.'

He closed his eyes. 'It certainly feels like it.'

'No wonder you shut people out,' Louisa said quietly. 'It must have been awful because no one truly understood what you were going through.'

'I'm not looking for sympathy, Louisa,' he said heavily. 'What happened, happened. We should have ended our relationship a long time before we did. Melissa was right, I wasn't any good at marriage.'

'She said that? And you believed her?' Louisa was horrified. 'She's the one who had the affair, Mac.'

'Because I was too busy to pay her any attention.' He stared into the dying embers of the fire. 'I hardly ever came home.'

'She wasn't here, Mac. She was up in London, building her career. What was there for you to come home to?'

'I could have moved to London.'

'You've got the sea in your soul, Mac Sullivan. You could never live in any city and Melissa must have known that. I expect she thought she could change you,' Louisa said sagely. 'People often think that about other people. Weird really.'

He looked at her with a faint smile. 'And what about you? Do you think that?'

She shook her head. 'If you're asking me if I'd want to change you, the answer is no,' she said softly. 'I love the fact that your job means so much to you, that you care so much. It's part of the man you are. I love the fact that you love the sea. I just wish you'd talk to me a bit more. Not because I want to change the way you are but because I think you've shut yourself away long enough. It's time to let people back into your life, Mac. Time to move on.'

There was a long, pulsing silence while they watched each other, trapped by the rising tension that swirled and twisted around them.

Louisa could see the battle in his eyes, read the indecision. So she made the decision for both of them. With a courage she hadn't known she possessed, she slid along the sofa and wound her arms round his neck.

'Kiss me, Mac.' Her voice was husky and her eyes were on his mouth. 'Make love to me like you did last night.'

She could sense the struggle inside him and then he cursed under his breath and unlocked her arms from around his neck. 'No, Louisa.' He stood up suddenly, his breathing unsteady, his eyes tormented. 'It wouldn't work. I'm totally wrong for you and I'll hurt you.'

'Mac—'

'We're different, Louisa. You like crowds and company, I like solitude.'

'Sometimes I like solitude, too,' she said softly, 'and sometimes you like crowds and company. It's just that you've forgotten how to just relax and enjoy yourself.'

'I can't offer you a relationship. I'm hopeless at relationships. I'm too selfish.' He gave a humourless smile. 'I'm obsessed with my work.'

'It wasn't that you were bad at relationships, Mac.' Louisa stared at the lights flickering on the tree. 'It's just that you were in the wrong one. But you and I have a chance of happiness. We should take it, even if it's only for tonight.'

'No.' He shook his head. 'That isn't what you need. You've said it yourself, Louisa—you're waiting for the fairy-tale. Well, I'm not anyone's idea of a fairy-tale.'

CHAPTER TEN

LOUISA awoke to find Hopeful lying on the bed next to her, a sorrowful expression on his face.

Her first thought was that it shouldn't have been Hopeful.

It should have been Mac.

But when did life ever turn out the way you wanted it to?

She reached out a hand and stroked his soft coat. 'You shouldn't be on the bed,' she murmured as she forced herself awake. 'If Mac found out he'd be furious and there'd be another black mark against you.'

She glanced at the clock and gave a gasp. 'Oh, my goodness!' She scrambled out of bed in a sudden panic, her dark hair falling over her face and the strap of her nightdress trailing down her arm. 'I need to check the turkey.'

Picking up on her panic, Hopeful leaped off the bed with an excited bark, his tail wagging so hard that his whole body was moving.

'Louisa.' A deep voice from the doorway made her freeze and she looked at Mac in horror.

There was no way of hiding Hopeful.

'I can explain—'

His gaze rested on Hopeful. 'That dog obviously isn't as stupid as he looks.'

She gave a weak smile. 'I would have preferred to share the bed with you.'

Dark eyes clashed with hers. 'We're too different, Louisa. I can't make you happy.'

'I think you'd make me very happy,' she said softly, dragging the strap of her nightdress back up her arm. 'I just think you're too afraid to risk another relationship. But you need to realise that Melissa was just the wrong woman for you. It was a mistake. It happens to people all the time. If you'd spent more time together you probably would have realised sooner.'

He stared at her. 'I preferred to work.'

She gave a soft smile, wondering how such an intelligent man could be so obtuse. 'And why was that, Mac? One day when you're having a few hours off from blaming yourself and taking responsibility for everything, you should try asking yourself that question.'

He inhaled sharply and took a step backwards, his gaze shuttered. 'I have to go into work now.'

Avoiding the issue again.

She blinked and brushed her hair away from her face. 'It's Christmas morning, Mac, and you're supposed to be off until tomorrow. People are coming here to spend the day with us. I'm cooking turkey and there are presents round the tree.'

And mistletoe above the doorways.

She was doing a proper Christmas.

He looked as though she'd suggested he run naked down the coast road. 'They're really busy. Short of staff. I need to go in.'

He wanted to go in.

She felt the hope drain out of her.

Clearly he was willing to do anything to avoid

Christmas. *To avoid being with her.* 'You're going to the hospital?'

She couldn't quite believe it. *Didn't want to believe it.*

'It's my job, Louisa.' He turned and strode away, leaving her staring after him with tears in her eyes and the smell of turkey wafting up the stairs.

'It's your job, Mac,' she said softly, 'but not your life.'

Mac watched while Josh intubated the patient and secured the airway, his movements smooth and proficient. He felt a burn of pride that went right to the bone. *His kid brother was a hell of a doctor.*

When exactly had he moved from eager junior doctor to cool-headed, experienced consultant? He was a team member to be proud of. *A brother to be proud of.*

Suddenly Mac found that he had a lump in his throat. *What was happening to him?* He struggled to concentrate. 'I want all his clothes removed so that we can do a proper assessment...' He went through the moves like clockwork, part of him detached from what was happening around him. 'X-rays.' He glanced at Sue, his face blank of expression. 'Let's start with lateral cervical spine, chest and pelvis.'

It was Christmas Day.

All around the country families were getting together, ripping open presents, sharing joy, arguing and eating too much. Some people were on their own and longing to find someone to share the day with.

For him it was just another day in A and E.

Another road traffic accident victim to be patched up.

He stared down at the patient on the trolley and suddenly all he could see was Louisa's wide smile and all he could think about was her unshakable optimism and her generosity towards everyone and everything.

Then he glanced up and took in the cold sterility of the resuscitation room where he seemed to spend most of his days. Harsh lights shone down on the patient, illuminating the cruelty of fate, the fragility of life. Chrome glinted and the paint on the functional white walls was starting to chip in places where it had been bashed by trolleys with sharp edges. The place was stark, sterile and cold. *The last place that anyone should be spending Christmas if there was an alternative.*

And he had an alternative.

1   What the hell was he doing here when he could be at home surrounded by Louisa's warmth?

He shook himself and tried to concentrate again. Still functioning on automatic, he checked the femoral pulses. 'Let's do a serum amylase…'

What was it that brought him here day after day? Night after long night?

He pushed the thought away impatiently as he examined the patient's peritoneum. What the hell was the matter with him? He loved his work and apart from the beach there was no place he'd rather be. That was why he was standing here on Christmas Day instead of lounging at home eating too much of Louisa's undoubtedly delicious turkey.

'There's bruising over the abdomen, Mac.'

He suddenly realised that they were looking at him expectantly, waiting for him to make decisions, give orders.

Trying to ignore the thoughts clouding his brain, he did what was expected of him, going through the motions, relying on years of training and experience to guide him in the right direction.

He didn't want to be here.

He remembered Louisa with her arms round a muddy Hopeful, worried to death that a strange, abandoned dog might be hurt. He remembered her offering to cook lunch for Alice and inviting Rick, a stranger, to bring his little girl to sit by their tree on Christmas Day. He remembered her in high heels and an evening dress, covering a badly injured boy with her coat while she risked hypothermia. *He remembered the way she'd given herself to him without reservation.*

Something shifted inside him and the clouds in his brain suddenly cleared. When he'd been married to Melissa, Christmas had just been another day of work. And he'd thought that had said everything about the man he was.

Now he realised that it said everything about his relationship.

Louisa was right.

He stared at the X-rays.

'Call the surgeons,' Josh instructed, his blue eyes fixed on his brother's face and then moving back to the X-rays. 'He needs a laparotomy and he needs it now. Mac, go home. I can cope here now. For once you're supposed to be off duty. My gift to you is waiting at home and I think it's time you went and appreciated it. Merry Christmas.'

Mac blinked and realised that his brother was covering for him. 'I'm fine.'

'Go and eat Louisa's turkey.' It was an order. Quietly spoken, but an order just the same.

Mac looked at his younger brother, *the brother he loved*, and they shared a look of complete understanding.

It was finally time to move on.

Mac stepped back from the trolley and ripped off his gloves.

With a final look at his brother, Josh turned his attention back to the patient. 'Bleep the surgeons again and let's give him cefuroxime IV. What are his sats?'

Mac walked towards the door without a backward glance. Behind him the team closed round the patient, each carrying out his or her own tasks.

It was Christmas Day.

And he was going home.

'I can't believe he went to work.' Her face pink from the heat of the Aga, Louisa blew wisps of hair out of her eyes and struggled to lift the turkey onto a different surface. 'It means I'm going to have to carve and I'm useless at carving.'

Alice looked up from her third glass of sweet sherry. 'Well, I'd love to help, dear, but I've only got the one wrist and frankly I wasn't that great at carving when I had two.'

Louisa gave a weak smile as she transferred the turkey to a carving tray. Hopeful bashed against her legs, wagging his tail. She glanced down. 'I suppose if I drop this, that will solve the problem of carving it. Get away, darling, I'll feed you in a minute.'

For her the sparkle of Christmas had dimmed the moment Mac had strode out of the house that morning.

There was a ring on the doorbell and seconds later Hannah danced into the kitchen, a pair of antlers fixed to her blonde hair, her cheeks pink from the cold.

'They let me off early!!' She flung her jacket over the nearest chair, revealing a tight pair of jeans and a sparkly top. She cast a look over her shoulder and then looked back at Louisa. 'Where is he? Rick?'

Her eyes shone and Louisa smiled. 'In the sitting room with Poppy. Go and find them.'

She looked at the soft look on Hannah's face and decided that maybe her Christmas hadn't been such a disaster after all. She was pleased for them both. And it would be lovely for Poppy.

Louisa was dying to ask how Mac had been but she didn't dare.

He wasn't here, she reminded herself.

That was all she needed to know.

'It will be ready soon.'

'Louisa, can I play with Hopeful?' Poppy bounded into the kitchen, clutching a large bunch of mistletoe, Rick close on her heels, his expression brightening as he spotted Hannah.

'Great to see you.'

Hannah blushed and scooped an excited Poppy into her arms. 'Shall we take that dog into the sitting room and play with him?'

'I wish you would,' Louisa said fervently, vowing that next year she was going to study the anatomy of a turkey so that she could carve the thing herself. 'I can't think about him at the moment. I need to do the sprouts.'

Poppy screwed up her face. 'I hate sprouts.'

'You're supposed to hate sprouts,' Alice said happily from her seat at the kitchen table. Her cheeks were flushed from the alcohol. 'You're a child. All children hate sprouts.'

'You won't hate my sprouts.' Louisa checked the bread sauce, put the cranberry on the heat to warm and stirred the gravy. 'We can eat in ten minutes.'

'Great,' Hannah said cheerfully. 'I'm starving.'

Alice looked shocked. 'But Mac isn't home yet.'

Louisa paused, the hand that was stirring the gravy suddenly still. 'He isn't coming home, Alice,' she mumbled, cursing under her breath as she felt tears clog her throat. Oh, she was so stupid! *She'd frightened him away.* She'd let him see how much she loved him and that had frightened him away.

He was at the hospital again because of *her*.

And hadn't the whole purpose of her visit been to persuade Mac to share Christmas with the world? Maybe he would have done that if she hadn't been so stupid as to fall in love with him.

Josh would be so disappointed in her.

She was disappointed in herself. Not for falling in love with Mac—*she couldn't have stopped that*—but for showing him how she felt, for putting pressure on him when he so clearly didn't feel the same way.

She was old enough to know that men could have sex, even tremendous sex, without feeling anything emotionally. To the best of her knowledge, Josh had been doing it for most of his adult life. She'd been naïve to think that it had meant something more to Mac.

And because of her, *because of the things she'd said*, he'd gone to work when he should have been in his own home.

She'd made things worse, instead of helping.

Pushed him too far in her clumsy attempt to help.

Swamped by guilt and worry for Mac, she surreptitiously wiped her eyes on her sleeve.

'Poppy…' Alice's voice was remarkably firm, given the volume of sherry she'd consumed. 'That's Hopeful's lead on that peg—just over there. Take him down to the beach for five minutes, dear. Daddy and Hannah will go with you. Wrap up warm. It's freezing out there.'

Rick glanced at Louisa and then at the old lady, saw something in her eyes and gave a nod. 'Great idea. We'll get some fresh air before lunch. Get out from under your feet. Come on, Poppy.'

They vanished from the kitchen and Louisa and Alice were left alone.

'Hannah and Rick seem quite taken with each other,' Louisa said brightly, stirring the gravy vigorously and making a supreme effort to pull herself together.

Life wasn't about fairy-tale endings.

She should know that better than anyone.

Life was hard and challenging and full of things you wanted and couldn't have.

Like love and a family.

Like Mac.

'Now, dear.' Alice's voice was soft. 'Leave that gravy to simmer, sit down at this table and tell me what exactly has been happening between you and our lovely Dr Sullivan?'

Louisa dropped the spoon and turned to look at her, her expression stricken. 'I did all the wrong things—said all the wrong things. I've driven him out of his own home. I wanted to make everything better, Alice, and instead I've just made everything ten times worse.'

And she felt *horribly* guilty.

Alice shook her head. 'That's not true, dear. You're loving and kind. How can someone like you ever make anything worse?' She wrinkled her nose thoughtfully. 'We felt the same, you know. After his wife died. The whole community tried their best. It's hard, you know, finding the right thing to say, and I don't think any of us managed it. He thought we were interfering.'

'I don't think he wanted to hear it,' Louisa mumbled, giving up on the gravy and rummaging in her sleeve for a tissue. 'He didn't think he deserved sympathy.'

'Because he blamed himself.' Alice sighed. 'But he had no reason to. That was never a marriage made in heaven. Anyone could see that.'

'Except him.' Louisa collapsed onto the nearest chair and dropped her head onto her arms. 'I'm so tired I could fall asleep on the spot. All I know is I've created this busy, noisy, merry Christmas and he doesn't want it. I'm sitting here, surrounded by turkey and a tree, just dying for him to come home, and he doesn't want any of it. He's at the hospital, patching up patients. And it's my fault. If I wasn't here he could come home and enjoy Christmas in his own way. He wanted to be on his own and I should have just let him. But I had to interfere.'

'And a good thing, too. You're the right girl for him,' Alice said gruffly, 'and I know that he's going to see that, Louisa. You have to hang on, dear.'

Louisa shook her head despondently. Where Mac was concerned she'd run out of energy and given up hope, and suddenly she just wanted to cry like a child. She lifted her head and bit her lip.

'It's like making a cake with no recipe,' she choked, struggling to hold back the tears. 'I've got all the right ingredients but I've done something wrong in the mixing. He doesn't want me, Alice. And nothing I do can change that. He doesn't want anyone. Perhaps he never will.'

With a cluck of sympathy, Alice moved round the table and scooped Louisa into her arms. 'There, sweetie, have a good cry…'

It felt good to be held and for a moment Louisa was tempted to just snuggle against Alice and have a good howl.

But then she smelt the turkey.

'I can't.' She gave a massive sniff and wiped her nose on her sleeve. 'I've got a turkey to carve and I can't do that with blurred vision. I can't even do it with perfect vision. I'm hopeless with knives.'

'We'll do it together,' Alice promised, and Louisa gave a wobbly smile.

'You've had three sherries, Alice.' She blew her nose hard. 'Your carving will be worse than mine and, knowing our luck, you'll end up in A and E, having chopped your finger off.'

'Well, at least then we'd see Mac,' Alice pointed out with a girlish giggle, and Louisa smiled.

'I don't think I want to go to those lengths for a date. You do cheer me up, Alice.'

'And you cheer me up, too, dear. In fact, you cheer everyone up, and if our Mac can't see that then he isn't the man I know him to be.' Alice gave her another hug and then sniffed the air. 'You might want to do something about that gravy. I think it's burning.'

'Oh, my goodness.' Louisa jumped to feet and hurried to the Aga to rescue the gravy, lifting it off the heat and pouring it into the jug she'd warmed in readiness. 'OK. I can't put this off any longer. I'm going to carve.' She lifted the tray and placed it in the middle of the kitchen table. 'Here goes.'

'I think I might need another sherry,' Alice said vaguely, as she stared at the bird.

'Not yet, Alice,' Louisa wailed, brandishing a knife. 'I need you sober to help me with this. Do you like red meat or white meat? Not that it makes much difference, the way I carve. It all sort of merges together.'

'Go for it,' Alice urged, reaching for the sherry bottle. 'I'm right behind you.'

Mac opened the door of his house and paused, a slight smile touching his hard mouth.

From the kitchen came delicious smells and he could hear shrieks of laughter. And it felt good. His house was filled with life.

And then he realised that his house wasn't just filled with life, it was filled with Louisa.

Suddenly he couldn't wait to get her on her own but he knew how much she wanted to share it with her new friends. And her generosity towards almost total strangers was what made her the woman he loved.

And he did love her.

He knew that now.

A smile on his lips, he walked quietly through to the conservatory, which was laid for Christmas lunch. There was something he needed to do before he told them he was here.

Five minutes later he pushed open the kitchen door, his eyes taking in the scene. Alice was dancing with Rick, Hannah was watching them from her seat at the kitchen table and Poppy was chasing the dog, waving a piece of mistletoe.

'Kiss me, Hopeful—please, kiss me—'

A grin on his face, Mac reached down and grabbed the dog by his collar. 'When a lady asks you for a kiss, it's a good idea to comply. Sit!'

'Mac!' Delight exploding across her face, Louisa dropped the bowl she was holding and it smashed on the floor. 'Oh, no! Those were my sprouts!'

She was pleased to see him.

More than pleased.

The look on her pretty face gave him the biggest high he could ever remember having.

'Oh, great.' Poppy jumped up and down with glee as she surveyed the remains of the vegetables. 'I hate sprouts. I really hate them.'

'But my sprouts are delicious,' Louisa protested, dropping to her knees and trying to clear up the mess.

Hopeful stuck his nose in the mess and Louisa gave him a push. 'You can't eat these—you'll have a stomachache.'

'And my credit card can't stand another trip to the vet's,' Mac drawled, walking across to the kitchen and hauling Louisa to her feet. 'Leave the sprouts,' he ordered huskily. 'I'll clear it up in a minute.'

He wanted to kiss her, but he knew that everyone was watching and she already looked flustered enough. He'd never seen Louisa flustered in the kitchen before.

'What are you doing home?' She wiped her hands on the front of her jeans, adorably self-conscious. 'I thought you weren't coming home.'

'I heard that someone around here was cooking a turkey.' He stared down into her sweet face and suddenly nothing in his life had ever seemed so clear. 'Without sprouts.'

'Actually, there's another bowl of sprouts in the Aga.'

Poppy groaned. 'Oh, no.' She flung her arms round Hopeful. 'I wish I was you. No one makes a dog eat sprouts.'

Mac stared at the kitchen table and did a double-take. 'Louisa?' His voice was faint. 'What happened to the turkey?'

'Me. That's what happened to it.' She pulled a face and gave an awkward shrug. 'I told you that I'm not that great at carving.'

'Carving?' He struggled not to laugh. 'You *carved* that? It looks as though it was caught in helicopter blades.'

Her face drooped. 'I don't think I've ever really grasped the anatomy of a turkey,' she confessed sadly. 'I'm sure it will taste fine. It's the same bird.'

'It was a bird?' Mac couldn't hold back the smile. 'I think next year I'd better carve.'

He saw Louisa's startled look. The question in her eyes. The hope.

Suddenly he longed to drag her down to the beach and tell her that he was going to be carving her turkey for the rest of his life, but then he noticed Alice sway.

'Are you all right?' He frowned sharply and Alice gave a girlish giggle.

'Oh, I'm fine,' she said gaily. 'Just enjoying a dance with this handsome young man.'

Rick grinned and helped her to the nearest chair. 'You're pretty nimble on your feet, Alice,' he said, and Louisa threw a pleading glance at Mac.

'She's had too much sherry on an empty stomach,' she muttered, surreptitiously sliding the bottle away from Alice. 'We need to eat before she passes out. Let's get to the table and I can serve.'

'I haven't passed out from drink since I was a girl,' Alice said cheerfully, flopping onto the chair, 'so don't worry about me.'

Mac strolled up to the table and offered his arm. 'Let's go through to the conservatory,' he suggested, his eyes resting on Louisa, who was hurrying around the kitchen like a mad thing, putting the finishing touches to the lunch. 'I popped in on Vera before I came home and she was enjoying herself hugely. She had three doctors perched on the end of her bed, listening to her wartime stories.'

Alice laughed. 'Poor things.' She swayed slightly and caught Mac's arm. 'Come on, then, let's sit down.'

Louisa stared at her plate and suddenly realised that she wasn't hungry. Her insides were too churned up to eat.

Why had Mac come home?

And what had he meant by that comment about carving the turkey from now on?

Nothing, she told herself firmly. He meant nothing. And she wasn't going to fall into the trap of imagining a fondness that wasn't there.

She glanced out of the window.

Beyond the conservatory windows the garden was white from a new fall of snow and beyond that the sea stretched, gunmetal grey, into the distance.

Next week she'd be back in London.

Back to her anonymous life in an anonymous city.

The thought depressed her beyond belief.

'Louisa…' Alice's voice came from the far end of the table. 'You haven't pulled your cracker, dear.'

Louisa gave a determined smile. She had to join in. She didn't want to spoil anyone else's Christmas Day by being a misery. She glanced around her. 'I can't find my cracker—that's weird. I'm sure I put one out for everyone.'

'It's here.' Mac lounged next to her, his dark gaze intent on her face. He was holding her cracker.

Louisa took the cracker and forced a smile. 'All right—who is going to pull this one with me. Poppy?'

'Not Poppy.' Mac's voice was deep and his eyes held hers. 'Me.'

She hid her surprise. He wanted to pull a cracker

with her? He really was getting into the Christmas spirit.

'All right but I ought to warn you that I hate the bang.' She curled her fingers around the cracker and instinctively closed her eyes. Then she pulled.

There was a bang and a metallic clatter as something fell onto her side plate.

Everyone around the table fell silent and Louisa opened her eyes and glanced around her. 'What's the matter with you lot? Have you—?' She looked down at her plate and gave a gasp.

A beautiful diamond ring lay on her plate, sparkling like the decorations on the Christmas tree.

She stared at in stunned silence.

In disbelief.

Hannah gave a gasp and Alice gave a sigh. 'It's amazing, the quality of crackers these days. For a moment I thought that ring was real.'

Louisa reached out and touched the ring hesitantly, as if it might disappear at any time. A huge diamond twinkled and glinted and she stared down at it in fascination.

What did it mean? *She didn't dare hope…*

'Are you going to look at me, Louisa?' Mac's voice was rough and gentle at the same time, and suddenly she couldn't breathe properly.

'Mac…' She knew she shouldn't hope and yet she couldn't stop herself. And she couldn't look at him in case he saw that hope and killed it.

'I'm sorry I wasn't here to carve the turkey,' he said softly, taking her shaking hand in his and holding it firmly, 'but next year I will be and for every year after that unless I'm required at the hospital. But if that happens, we'll cook our turkey on Boxing Day instead.'

She lifted her eyes to his, oblivious to the fact that they had an audience. 'What are you saying?'

He smiled and picked up the ring, sliding it onto her finger. 'I'm saying that you're the best Christmas present that my brother has ever given me, and I intend to keep you. I'm saying that I love you.' His voice was husky and there was a smile in his eyes. 'I think I've probably loved you since the moment you fell through my toilet window, but I was too blind to see it.'

She stared at the ring in wonder and felt something lodge in her throat. 'You don't do relationships.'

'That was before I met you,' Mac said huskily. 'Now I've discovered that I was wrong. I went into the hospital and for the first time in my life I didn't want to be there. I wanted to be here. With you.'

There was another sigh from Alice. 'That's *so* romantic.'

Without turning, Mac grinned. 'Thank you, Alice.' He tightened his grip on Louisa's hand. 'Are you going to speak?'

'I was afraid I'd driven you away.'

'You've given me my life back.' He slid his other hand around the back of her neck and pulled her gently towards him. 'You've made me see things as they really are.'

'Are they going to kiss?' Poppy stared at them in fascination and then glanced at her father. 'Are they going to kiss?'

Rick grinned and scratched his head. 'Looks like

they might. Close your eyes, sweetie. Perhaps you shouldn't be watching.'

Louisa blushed and Mac gave a slow smile of masculine satisfaction. 'No kissing. In a moment we're going for a long walk on the beach and there will definitely be some kissing then, but for now I just want Louisa to answer one very important question.'

Alice cleared her throat. 'Is there any more gravy?'

Mac closed his eyes briefly. 'I'm trying to propose, Alice.'

'Oh, goodness.' Alice turned pink and adjusted her paper hat, which was falling over her eyes. '*Do* carry on. I'm not saying another word. Not another word.'

Louisa started to giggle, happiness erupting inside her. 'Mac…'

Mac took a deep breath and then Hopeful crashed into the room, the remains of the turkey in his mouth.

Louisa gave a gasp of horror and stood up. 'Oh, Mac! He's got a turkey bone! It will splinter in his mouth and we'll have to take him to the vet!'

'Hopeful!' There was no mistaking the authority in Mac's tone and the dog stopped on the spot and dropped the bone.

'Oh!' Louisa stared at him in delight. 'He's learning to be obedient! You wonderful dog. I hope you didn't swallow any, darling.' She was on her knees beside the dog, sliding her fingers into his mouth to check. 'I think he's OK.'

'I'm relieved to be spared the experience of discovering how much vets charge on Christmas Day,' Mac said dryly. 'And now, if no one minds, I'm taking Louisa down to the beach for a walk so that I can propose in peace.'

'I know she'll say yes,' Alice said wisely, 'so shall we have another drink to celebrate?'

Hannah giggled. 'Alice, you're going to be under the table.'

'Probably.' Alice reached for her glass. 'Just make sure you wake me up for the Queen's speech.'

The beach was deserted and the sky was grey and threatening.

'There's going to be more snow.' Louisa glanced upwards and Mac caught her in his arms and pulled her against him.

'I don't want to talk about the weather,' he growled, 'and I don't want to talk about turkey, Alice or Hopeful. I just want to talk about us and that ring you're wearing on your finger. And I need to do it quickly before there are any more interruptions. Will you marry me?'

He was strong, handsome and the embodiment of every dream she'd ever had.

Despite the cold, her insides melted. 'I can't believe you really love me,' she whispered as she stared up at him. *This couldn't be happening.* 'I'd given up hoping.'

'Well, I do love you. Madly. And you were right about so many things,' he said gruffly, stroking her cheek with his hand. 'And it's because of what I feel for you that I finally understand that what I had with Melissa wasn't right. When I was with Melissa I never once had this burning urge to come home. I was happier at the hospital.'

Louisa didn't notice the biting wind or the whisper of snow against her cheeks. 'And now?'

'I'll be happy wherever you are,' he said softly, lifting a hand and brushing her hair away from her face. 'Melissa and I were totally wrong for each other. If I'd loved her or she'd loved me, I would have followed her to London or she would have followed me to Cornwall. We would have wanted to be together. But the pull wasn't strong enough. I know that now. I didn't know what love was until I met you, but you taught me.'

She slid her arms round his neck. 'And what is love, Dr Sullivan?'

He cupped her face in his hands, lowered his mouth to hers and kissed her gently. 'Love is what I feel for you.' He muttered the words against her mouth, his touch warm and seductive. 'Love is wanting to be with someone and build a future together. Love is about creating a family and family traditions. Every Christmas from now on I will be home to carve the turkey. And every Christmas we will have a walk on the beach, just the two of us.'

She chuckled, her body trembling from his kiss. 'We won't need to. We won't have Alice every year.'

His mouth still hovered above hers. 'No, but it's the only way we'll get any peace from our five children.' His dark eyes gleamed. 'It was five, wasn't it, Louisa?'

She felt emotion welling up inside her. 'And a dog, Mac,' she said softly. 'Don't forget the dog.'

As if on cue, there was wild barking and Hopeful came loping across the sand towards them.

Mac glanced over his shoulder and raised his eyes to heaven. 'Somehow I don't think I'm going to be allowed to forget the dog. What does a guy have to do to propose in peace?' He turned back to her, laughter in his dark eyes. 'Quickly. Before he gets here and does something that requires another visit to the vet. Will you marry me?'

Hopeful bounded up to them, leaping and jumping, his tail wagging so hard he almost lost his balance.

Suddenly the world seemed perfect.

'Yes.' A smile spread across her face. 'I'll definitely marry you. Merry Christmas, Mac.'

'Merry Christmas.'

And he bent his head and kissed her.

MILLS & BOON®

1105/03b

Live the emotion

_MedicaL
romance™

THE NOBLE DOCTOR *by Gill Sanderson*

From the moment she meets gorgeous Dr Marc
Duvallier, midwife Lucy Stephens is sure he's The
One – and he's just as sure, just as quickly! But
Marc isn't only a doctor, he's also the Comte de
Montreval. Soon he must return home – can he ask
Lucy to leave her life behind for him?

*DELL OWEN MATERNITY: Midwives, doctors, babies
– at the heart of a Liverpool hospital*

A SURGEON WORTH WAITING FOR *by
Melanie Milburne*

Trauma surgeon Jack Colcannon and adorable
Dr Becky Baxter have a difficult relationship
– their brief affair ten years ago only adds to the
complication of them working together. Then Becky
becomes the target of terrifying threats and only
Jack can keep her safe – day and night…

*A&E DRAMA: Pulses are racing in these
fast-paced dramatic stories*

CHRISTMAS-DAY FIANCÉE *by Lucy Clark*

Dr Marty Williams, the new paediatric registrar,
is causing quite a stir – he's an excellent doctor,
gorgeous, funny and single – and he intends to stay
that way! Until Dr Natalie Fox re-enters his life.
Marty knows her better than anyone – and he also
knows why she has never let herself fall in love…

On sale 2nd December 2005

*Available at most branches of WHSmith, Tesco, ASDA,
Borders, Eason, Sainsbury's and most bookshops*

Visit www.millsandboon.co.uk

Make your Christmas wish list – and check it twice!

Watch out for these very special holiday stories – all featuring the incomparable charm and romance of the Christmas season.

By Jasmine Cresswell, Tara Taylor
Quinn and Kate Hoffmann
On sale 21st October 2005

By Lynnette Kent and
Sherry Lewis
On sale 21st October 2005

By Lucy Monroe and
Louise Allen
On sale 4th November 2005

By Heather Graham,
Lindsay McKenna, Marilyn
Pappano and Annette Broadrick
On sale 18th November 2005

By Marion Lennox, Josie Metcalfe
and Kate Hardy
On sale 2nd December 2005

By Margaret Moore, Terri Brisbin
and Gail Ranstrom
On sale 2nd December 2005

By Lisa Jackson, Barbara Boswell
and Linda Turner
On sale 18th November 2005

1105/059/MB146

Experience the magic of Christmas, past and present...

Christmas Brides

Don't miss this special holiday volume – two captivating love stories set in very different times.

THE GREEK'S CHRISTMAS BRIDE
by Lucy Monroe
Modern Romance

Aristide Kouros has no memory of life with his beautiful wife Eden. Though she's heartbroken he does not remember their passion for each other, Eden still loves her husband. But what secret is she hiding that might bind Aristide to her forever – whether he remembers her or not?

MOONLIGHT AND MISTLETOE
by Louise Allen
Historical Romance – Regency

From her first night in her new home in a charming English village, Hester is plagued by intrusive "hauntings." With the help of her handsome neighbour, the Earl of Buckland, she sets out to discover the mystery behind the frightful encounters – while fighting her own fear of falling in love with the earl.

On sale 4th November 2005

Celebrate Christmas with the Fortunes!

Enjoy three classic stories with the Fortunes—a family whose Christmas legacy is greater than mere riches.

ANGEL BABY by Lisa Jackson
Lesley Bastian is so grateful to Chase Fortune for delivering her baby – but trying to penetrate the walls around Chase's heart is almost as challenging as motherhood!

A HOME FOR CHRISTMAS by Barbara Boswell
As CEO of a major corporation, Ryder Fortune has little time for romance – until his assistant Joanna Chandler works her way into his hardened heart…

THE CHRISTMAS CHILD by Linda Turner
Naomi Windsong's little girl is missing and only Hunter Fortune can find her. But will time prove to be Hunter's greatest enemy – and love his greatest challenge?

THE FORTUNES
The price of privilege—the power of family.

On sale 18th November 2005